SHE'S ALL ALONE

AN ARTEMIS BLYTHE MYSTERY THRILLER BOOK 5

GEORGIA WAGNER

Contents

1. Prologue: 1

2. Chapter One   6

3. Chapter Two   26

4. Chapter Three   35

5. Chapter Four   53

6. Chapter Five   63

7. Chapter Six   72

8. Chapter Seven   91

9. Chapter Eight   110

10. Chapter Nine   116

11. Chapter Ten   137

12. Chapter Eleven   153

13. Chapter Twelve   171

14. Chapter Thirteen   182

15. Chapter Fourteen   198

16. Chapter Fifteen   213

17. Chapter Sixteen   223

18. What's next for Artemis Blythe?   244

19. Also by Georgia Wagner   246

20. Also by Georgia Wagner   248

About the Author   251

Also By Georgia Wagner   252

Girl Under the Ice   253

PROLOGUE:

HEART POUNDING, AZIN KARTOV reclined in his red leather lounging chair, his back to the bookcase, a small glass of red wine in one hand. He swirled it a couple of times, pausing to inhale the pleasant aroma. All of it a show of course; he was a bundle of nerves. *She* was on her way. He turned his attention once more to the dusty, leatherbound book, forcing his mind to slow, to calm. The pages were well-worn and practically falling from the tome. He checked the clock above the mantelpiece.

The small house smelled faintly of salt and ash. The ash came from the well-used fireplace, which the two-week tenant before him had managed to clog according to the subletter. The salt odor, though, came from the ocean. He looked across the room, peering out the large double windows at the ocean beyond. The water lapped against the shore, cresting white before breaking against the land.

In his home country, the scent and sight of the ocean was a foreign thing.

It made him feel small, unimportant.

And yet... he couldn't help but gaze through the window at the waters, like some unrequited lover jilted by his mistress.

He wouldn't be here long, though. He'd come for the live portion of the blitz tournament. Already, following a week of matches, he'd made it into the final sixteen. In an attempt to stir up viewership, the chess organizers had decided to attempt something unique. A sort of knockout bracket for the final sixteen, styled after a European soccer league.

He shot another glance towards the clock, biting his lip briefly, shifting in his seat.

He glanced towards the door and heard the buzzer. Right on cue.

He smiled, feeling a tingle of nerves. They were on opposite sides of the brackets. Which was why he'd been able to schedule the meeting, so they could pick each other's brains about their opponents.

Of course, he was under no illusion about his chances against the current world champion. It had been pure bad luck that he'd drawn Anton Radesh in the first knockout round.

He called out now, "Door is open—just push!" He smiled, swirling his wine some more, taking a sip then lowering it onto an oak side table.

The door opened, and a woman stepped from the night tinged with ocean spray into his sublet. He smiled at her, nodding politely. She had dark hair, mismatched eyes—one the color of sky, the other like golden wheat. She was quite pretty but didn't wear makeup or jewelry. Her eyes were piercing though, and she stared at where he sat on the couch.

"As beautiful as you look in your profile picture," he said, going for something like charming, but his voice sounded thin to his ears. He took another sniff of the wine. "Hello, Artemis. How are you? A pleasure to meet again."

"Hello, Azin," the chess master replied sweetly. She approached. "Hopefully I didn't startle you by ringing the bell."

"No, no, not at all. I recognized you on the camera. See?" he pointed towards a small video screen above a couple of buttons by the door. "I knew you were coming, though, so I left the front door open."

Those entrancing, mismatched eyes studied him for a moment. "When was our last meeting? Two months ago, right? It's been awhile."

"Two months, yes. Seattle Open. You beat me quite handily with black." He chuckled. "Though, five months before that, a draw, remember?"

She laughed. "If I remember correctly, you started trading pieces by move three."

"Hmm, oh well," he said. "Strategies take time to arrange, don't they?"

"Yes. Well, should we get to it? I don't want to be up too late. Some of my friends are throwing a party for me at my friend's ranch." She shrugged sheepishly. "I told them I'd be a bit tardy, though."

"Of course, of course. My book of openings. I had three of them marked," Azin said, pointing down. He briefly lowered his eyes as well as his glass of wine.

"Azin?"

Something had changed in her voice.

"Azin?" she said, louder. "One other thing…"

He felt a tingle along his spine at the tone.

And then he looked up.

He went still.

"Artemis?" he said slowly, staring at the woman. "Ms. Blythe," he said, louder. "Wait—hey, hey!"

A gun was pointed at his head. She stood there, ice in her eyes, her posture one of complete defiance. "You knew this was coming, Azin," she murmured. "You had to know."

And then she pulled the trigger twice.

Two loud *bangs!*

Azin shot back, nearly tilting the red chair. It rocked on its heels from the momentum, then hit the ground again with a *thud.* He stared down, mouth open. He gaped at his chest, looked up, terror in his eyes. He looked down again, uttering a single strangled syllable. "Why?"

And he watched as two streams of blood burbled over his heart, pouring down his chest, along his stomach. He shifted once more, taking a shaking, hesitant breath. But his throat rasped as if the air had lodged somewhere.

He let out a final groan, and then his eyes fluttered, closing tight.

Darkness came quick.

The last image was of Artemis Blythe standing over him, gun still in her hand; she wore a red sweater with small white snowflakes stitched along the hems. She stared at him a moment longer, watching as crimson poured down his chest and dribbled onto the floor. Then she whispered.

"Sorry, Azin. But... one enemy at a time."

Chapter One

Artemis got out of the taxi under the watch of night. She gave a quick wave to the driver and then stepped onto the asphalt parking lot, adjusting her red sweater, which displayed small, white snowflakes along the hem. It wasn't exactly seasonal, seeing as they were still in autumn, but the sweater had been a gift from Sophie Kramer.

In fact, the Kramers were the ones throwing the celebratory party.

The driver was looking out at her, though, his car still idling. He watched her closely, frowning. "You're sure you're okay, ma'am?"

She gave a polite nod. "I'm fine, sir. Thank you." She forced a quick smile.

Of course, the truth was she wasn't fine. Not after the evening's events with Azin. It had ended so horribly. She gave a quick glance towards the taxi driver. "It's fine. Really."

"You looked distraught," he said carefully. "Was it... was it a man? Did he hurt you?" The taxi driver looked genuinely concerned, which only made her feel worse.

She remembered hurrying out of Azin's apartment, taking the stairs two at a time. Remembered pausing to throw that damn *thing* into the bushes. She'd been shaking badly, almost crying when the taxi had shown up.

Now, though, she'd calmed somewhat. She gave another quick smile. "Really, I'm fine. Thank you. Good night." She turned, facing the long driveway leading up to the ranch house, glowing with warm lights. She cleared her throat, took another step up the driveway, and tried to put the events of the night far from her mind. She'd done what she had to.

One enemy at a time. Her sister Helen used to say that. As Artemis moved up the long driveway, she couldn't help but think of her sister. The two of them had been inseparable for years, until Helen Blythe had disappeared at the age of fifteen.

One of the reasons Artemis now found herself back near Seattle was to investigate the disappearance.

In fact, she had been given something of a lead three weeks ago.

You want to find Helen? Ask your brother Tommy about the incident at the waterfall. About a year after you left.

She still shivered every time she remembered those words, especially because of the person who had uttered them. A man by the name of

John Kordan, one of the most notorious and prolific serial killers to have ever graced the Pacific Northwest with his presence.

The body count wasn't clear. But John and his mentor had been responsible for the murders of at least seventy people. Worse still, John had claimed students of his own. One of them, Artemis' father. She scowled, shivering at the recollection. At the way he had smiled then winked at her.

Even the memory left her feeling dirty.

But that was why she had come back to the ranch so quickly. At least, in part. She tried to shake the memory of what had happened back at that oceanside rental with Azin.

But this had been the only way to entice her brother out of his usual routine of avoiding her.

Tommy was involved with the Seattle mob. She had tried for the last few weeks to schedule something with him, but he had always found an excuse. Finally, she had asked Jamie Kramer, one of Tommy's oldest friends, to invite him to the ranch.

Jamie had agreed on one condition. That he was allowed to throw a celebratory party for Artemis.

The last few days had been a difficult combination of anticipating tonight, while playing in the blitz tournament. She hadn't prepared nearly as much as she had wanted, but thankfully, most of her matches had been below her skill level.

Now, having made the final sixteen, Jamie, and a few others he had invited, were waiting to celebrate her achievement.

Through the windows, she spotted streamers, purple and pink dangling in the windows. She spotted balloons, filled with helium, pressed against the ceiling, with long ribbons like tails.

She heard laughter and music. She thought she could smell the faint fragrance of barbecue.

Knowing Jamie, he had pulled out all the stops.

She spotted a couple of cars in the driveway. One of them she recognized, Jamie's. Another, black with tinted windows, suggested it likely belonged to one of her coworkers at the FBI.

But there was a third car she didn't recognize. She frowned, staring at the bright pink vehicle. A sedan. The last time she had seen a car the same color as Pepto-Bismol had been back in Chicago, in the form of a hatchback belonging to one of her favorite analysts, Cynthia Washington.

"You didn't," she muttered beneath her breath; she had expressly forbidden Jamie from inviting anyone out of state.

In fact, the person she had been trying to lure out of hiding hadn't come by car. He never did. She recognized the low rider motorcycle, though. Not so much the vehicle itself, but the mode of transportation.

The last time she had seen her brother, he had blown up a motorcycle he had stolen. She had doubts about the rightful ownership of this particular bike as well. A sleek, black thing with a seat resembling a skull.

"One enemy at a time," she muttered to herself.

She shifted uncomfortably, staring in the direction of the streamers and the balloons. The music continued to pulse through the house, playing some type of heavy metal, which she didn't doubt had been influenced by Tommy.

She reached the door, hand on the doorknob. And she paused.

She bit her lip, hesitant. She wasn't very accustomed to large gatherings of people. In fact, the only time she really participated in crowds was during chess tournaments. But then, she was allowed the excuse of focus to not mingle, engage in small talk, or shake everyone's hand, while forcing a wooden smile.

She was not much like Helen had been.

Helen had always been the more beautiful of the two. Helen had curly hair, where Artemis' was straight and black. Helen had been taller than Artemis, and she didn't have these damn mismatched eyes which everyone seemed to notice whenever Artemis entered the room. Helen's eyes had been a gentle lavender, like the flower.

Artemis missed her sister.

According to the Professor—the killer who'd escaped police custody three weeks ago by throwing acid into the eyes of FBI agents—Helen was *not* buried in the Cascade Mountains. That didn't mean she was alive.

But he'd given her a clue nonetheless. A clue she would see through tonight. *Ask your brother Tommy about the incident at the waterfall.*

She forced a fake smile, as was customary at events like this, and pushed open the door. She scanned the room and paused long enough to allow an actual smile to twist her lips.

A long picnic table had been set up in the middle of the room. Jamie Kramer was busy lighting candles on a large carrot cake. He waved a hand, clearing some of the ribbons dangling from the balloons on the ceiling.

Sophie, his little sister, had worn a cute, blue dress with a big bow in the back. She was skipping behind her older brother while occasionally stealing licks of frosting.

"Cut it," Jamie said after a second pilfering finger. "You're leaving marks!"

"Am not. Auntie Artemis doesn't mind."

Artemis winced at this nickname. Sophie had taken to calling her *auntie* when she visited. Given the nature of her relationship with Jamie, Artemis wasn't sure she liked being thought of this way.

Further in the room, sitting on a big, lumpy couch—which Jamie had sworn he was eventually going to rid himself of—Cynthia Washington and her husband Henry leaned back, speaking to one of Artemis' coworkers.

Artemis' eyebrows shot up. She stared in delight and surprise at the Washingtons. The last time she'd seen Cynthia had been back on the Fox River in Chicago. At the time, Henry had been despondent following the death of his grandson. But now, the pale-haired, smiling-eyed chess analyst was nodding along with something Artemis' coworker had said, waving a piece of cocktail shrimp about and sending droplets of red cocktail sauce flying despite his wife's best efforts.

Artemis gave a little sigh, trying to keep her smile affixed. She felt a strong sense of contentment, watching the Washingtons sit on that lumpy couch as they so often sat on their family couch when video-messaging her online. She could still picture, in her mind's eye, the tapestry of pictures drawn by their grandchildren hanging on the wall.

She also could easily remember how often she'd felt a tinge of jealousy when looking at the way the two older lovebirds leaned against each other or hooked their arms into one another's. As if each was a piece of the other. They'd been married for nearly forty years. She allowed her eyes to linger on the two analysts then move to Jamie Kramer where he was trying to keep one of the candles from drooping, while still defending the frosting from his nine-year-old sister.

Artemis' gaze moved to her coworkers. Agent Wade was the one in conversation with the Washingtons. The man was built a bit like a brick wall, with wide shoulders and thick muscles visible beneath the sleeves of his t-shirt. This was the first time, Artemis thought, she'd seen the man without a suit. He was wearing, however, his trademark sunglasses, even though it was night... indoors...

Forester, Wade's partner and all-around mischief-maker, leaned against a wall, fiddling with an eyepatch. He hated the thing. But after an incident with acid on the previous case, the doctors had told Agent Forester that if he wanted to fully recover the sight in his left eye, he needed to keep the eyepatch affixed for at least a month.

He had a week to go. She had it on good authority, like herself, Forester hated suits. He'd taken this opportunity, off work hours, to wear an obnoxious Hawaiian shirt with bright yellow flowers on a bright orange background. He had on flipflops and every few moments, as she listened, he tried to find an opportunity to mutter, "Aloha!" to anyone who'd listen. His hair was messy as ever, as if he'd just pushed out of bed. And the scar on the inside of his hand was visible now—especially due to the short sleeved Hawaiian shirt. She could see where the roping wound moved up his hand, his arm, towards the elbow. A surgery after a cage-fighting match in his youth according to Forester.

Then again, the man was a sociopath, so she wasn't always sure if he was telling her the truth.

She watched both the agents, feeling equal parts gratitude and discomfort. The gratitude was because they'd come to her celebration. She wasn't sure how Jamie had found their contact info, but she was glad to see the two feds there. They weren't exactly *friends,* but they'd been through some harrowing moments with one another, and it felt nice to have them show up.

The discomfort, however, came from the memories. She could still see the two men reeling about, clutching at their eyes and groaning in pain. Could picture the way Agent Wade had toppled from a chair after being shot twice in the chest by John Kordan.

For weeks, the police, the feds, everyone in the state, had searched for the serial killer.

News bulletins were still released. Rewards flashed across highway signs. But no one had found him. Search parties in the mountains hadn't located him either.

He was in the wind, having somehow escaped the hunt.

Artemis always felt something of a shiver as she remembered the pick-ax wielding, amateur prospector. He was out there, somewhere.

She could only hope that if she ever encountered him again, it was on the other side of thick bars in a maximum security prison. Maybe in the same prison as her old man—especially if the two had known each other years ago.

She forced such unhappy thoughts from her mind.

As she scanned the guests at the small party, she noticed the whole reason behind the celebration. Tommy Blythe. Her twin brother had never been much like her. Strategy games and years doing the same thing, hours and hours a day, was his version of hell. Tommy was a seat-of-his-pants, down and out scrapper, with more authority issues than a child movie star.

Like hers, his eyes were mismatched—one the color of wheat-fields, the other the hue of mountain streams. His, though, were opposite to hers, just like so many other things between them both.

Tommy was lean and scrawny, with spindly fingers. He also boasted a stupid face tattoo.

She frowned at the two words etched along his neck, under his chin and twirling up towards his ears. They were in a language she didn't understand, and the ink was fading. A single, teardrop streaked the corner of his left eye.

His long hair was pulled back in a ponytail which had been stored into the back of his leather jacket. He leaned back, watching the guests. Reserving looks of suspicion for the FBI agents. When Artemis had told her brother about her plan to train with the feds, he hadn't minded. But at the time he'd been dangling out of a hospital window. Now, in a more proximate scenario, he couldn't wipe the scowl off his face.

Artemis approached Tommy first, raising her hand in greeting.

He glanced over. Nodded once.

"Hey," she said softly, not wanting to gain everyone's attention at once.

"Sup," he replied.

"How are you?"

"Fine." He still wasn't smiling—he rarely did. Tommy often spoke in short, curt sentences. Not because he was stupid. But because every action, every choice Tommy made was a type of rebellion. His sisters had been smart, so he played the fool. His sisters had been academically gifted, so he went into sports. His father—before they'd found out what the man really was—had asked his children to learn to read people, to study body language. But the only bodies Tommy had studied had been those of semi-pretty classmates, usually the girlfriends of other students.

"Artemis!" Jamie exclaimed.

She turned, and this time didn't have to force a smile. Jamie hurried over to her, his sea-gray eyes, sat in a face bordering on the masculine side of pretty, with a straight jaw and high cheekbones. He reached out, embracing her quickly. He hesitated a second, though, and glanced down. "Oh, shit—was that me? Sorry... How's that cocktail sauce getting *everywhere*. I found some on the cake. Dammit."

Artemis followed his gaze. There was a stain of red on one of the snowflakes along her left arm. She frowned at the stain. Jamie tried to rub at it, but it wasn't coming out.

Meanwhile, Cynthia—who'd heard Jamie's outcry—had disarmed her husband of his flailing shrimp, saving the carpet from any more red droplets.

Jamie abandoned his ministrations on her sleeve and instead glanced up, smiling warmly. "Well, congratulations!" he said, beaming. He gestured towards the long table where a banner dangled over the edge, reading, *Congratulations, A!*

"A?" she said, amused.

"Yes... well, I tried to find all the letters, but..." he trailed off, wrinkling his nose. He leaned in as if to give her a quick peck on the cheek but paused suddenly, as if realizing they were in public, then quickly cleared his throat and retreated, yelling, "Sophie—what did I say! You've put out one of the candles now!"

Artemis' cheek tingled in anticipation of the kiss that never was.

There had been *other* kisses over the last couple of weeks. Each nearly as memorable as the one in the gazebo under the rain. Now, not only her cheek, but her lips were tingling strangely. She cleared her throat, giving a quick shake of her head. Luckily, the Washingtons saved her from her own embarrassment, both of them waving merrily in her direction.

"Hello, Artemis!" Mrs. Washington exclaimed, beaming happily. "Congratulations! I watched the last two games live—you were incredible!"

Henry nodded with his wife. "I didn't see that back row pin coming, to be honest. Way to go, Blythe!"

Artemis beamed at the two of them. "Thank you so much for coming! You shouldn't have."

"Nonsense," the Washingtons both said at the same time. Then they glanced at each other and, eyes twinkling, Cynthia's hand found her husband's, giving it a little squeeze.

Artemis wanted to say more, but she felt a quick tug on her arm. She glanced back. Tommy was frowning down at her. "What's this about?"

She blinked, turning to face him now. She could feel some of the eyes in the room still watching her. Agent Wade's eyes were hard to track behind those sunglasses. Agent Forester was still reclining near his partner, wearing that eye patch, pretending like he wasn't watching her. As Jamie Kramer passed, extending a cheese platter, Forester accepted one of the snacks but only frowned after Jamie as the man walked away.

Artemis returned her full attention to Tommy. "Umm, it's..." she paused, distracted. She rubbed absentmindedly at the red stain on her sweater. "It's a celebration. I made it to the round of sixteen."

"Hmm?"

"I've been playing in a chess tournament this week. I made it to the last sixteen."

"Oh. Huh. Good job." Tommy glanced at Jamie, frowning. "He said he needed my help. Said it was important." Tommy adjusted the sleeves of his leather jacket. "I probably should get going, sis."

"No, no, wait," she said hurriedly. "It's important you stay."

Tommy glanced at Wade then Forester. "Not exactly my crowd, Art."

"I know. But..." How best to broach the question? To simply ask it? To lead up to it? What had the killer meant. Was her brother hiding something from her? Did he know something about Helen she didn't?

"Umm... I actually wanted to ask you something, Tommy."

"What?"

"Well... maybe. Do you think you could join me in the kitchen?"

"Okay." He turned, striding towards the kitchen, past the marble divider between the rooms, and then settling against the stove, narrowly avoiding one of the heat knobs with his scrawny form.

She joined him as well, and as she moved away from the main room, some of the murmuring conversation and the background heavy metal music faded a bit. A few drinks had been left open in red cups on the counter. There was a second, backup cake with a note that read, *Don't touch. For party.*

By the looks of things, Jamie had also cleared the local market's chip aisle, having now moved them to his kitchen and stacking the potato chips and dips all along one corner, crammed against the fridge. Jamie always did have a way of pulling out all the stops.

Tommy was examining the chips then his sister. "So you two still banging?"

"What?" she stared at him.

"Just a question. Big pile of chips for someone he's not screwing."

"Tommy! No, we're not... we're not..." Artemis' cheeks warmed, and she turned away, staring at the ground for a moment. She glanced at the window overlooking the ranch and the penned in land. For a moment, along the road leading to the house, she thought she spotted dark shapes. She frowned, peering forward, but Tommy cleared his t hroat.

"You're acting strange, Art."

She looked back at him, her heart spiking with fear. She faced her brother, realizing that if ever there was a time to broach the subject, it was now. And so, she said, slowly... "I met someone... Someone very bad—very evil—recently. And... and he told me something."

Tommy didn't reply, just watched her from under hooded eyes.

"And..." Artemis trailed off for a moment, choosing her words carefully. "And he said I should ask you something. About Helen."

Tommy continued watching her, his long hair having somehow come untucked from the back of his leather jacket. His mismatched eyes fixated on hers. She couldn't read him. Tommy had grown up with the same father. He guarded his body language, the emotional tics just as much as he guarded his words. Curt with language and curt with emotion—she wasn't quite sure how her brother managed it. But he did.

And so she said, simply, "What happened at the waterfall? A year after I left?"

It was as if she'd cast a spell. Tommy's expression flickered and suddenly darkened, as if a storm had passed behind his eyes. He frowned at her now. "Who have you been talking to?"

"So something *did* happen?" she said, excitedly.

"Who?"

"A murderer by the name of John Kordan. He escaped police custody three weeks ago and is currently at large. Now you answer my question."

He looked away, refusing to meet her gaze now. Which for a stubborn, stiff-necked man like her brother was essentially an admittance of some type of guilt. Though what type of guilt? His long fingers tapped against each other—he wore fingerless gloves as he so often did, and for a moment, it looked as if he was keeping rhythm with the music from the other room.

"Like the tunes?" he asked after a moment. "Jamie let me choose."

"I figured as much. Tommy, what's going on?"

"Dunno. This is your party."

"What happened at the waterfall? *What* waterfall?"

"Dunno."

"Tommy!" she said, exasperated.

Her brother looked back at her, and for a moment, she spotted something in his gaze that was unfamiliar to her.

Something that she had rarely seen show up in her brother's countenance.

Fear.

He shook his head once. Then, he murmured, quietly, "If I told you… you wouldn't believe me," he said. "What I don't know is how this killer of yours knows anything happened. Is Dad involved?" Tommy said suddenly, glaring. "He is, isn't he? Artemis, you know better than to play games with that bastard!"

"Tommy, just answer the question! What happened at the waterfall? The one near Pinelake? Is that right?"

"What happened, Artemis, is that nothing happened. Not really. Now just let it go. Don't get sucked in. This is what Dad wants."

"Dad had nothing to do with this."

"Bullshit."

"It's true!" She realized a second later that she'd snagged her brother's arm and was holding on tight.

He glanced down at where she gripped his wrist, frowning. He gave a little tug, pulling his arm away. "Artemis," he said firmly, "if some weird psycho is asking you questions, then Dad is involved. You and I both know it. Let it go. Let this go."

"Why? Why won't you just tell me?"

Tommy was growing angry now, or perhaps he was simply matching the energy in her tone. As he began to raise his voice, his cheeks tinged red, he went still. He frowned.

And then Artemis realized his cheeks *really* were tinged red. Except, it was coming from the lights flashing through the windows. Red and blue flashed over Tommy's visage. She stared at her brother, but he was staring out the windows.

"Shit—Art, you turning me in?" he demanded.

Artemis shook her head, mouth open, staring out the window at the approaching police vehicles. Nearly six of them, all speeding towards the ranch house.

Six cop cars?

What for?

She heard sudden buzzing now, ringing. And she glanced over towards where Forester and Wade were looking at their phones. Wade frowned first, Forester leaned in, showing his phone to his partner as if double-checking he had the right thing on his screen.

The two of them stared at Forester's screen a moment, and then they both looked up, gaping at Artemis.

She felt as if she'd been suddenly pinned to the floor. Forester's patched eye and Wade's sunglasses served to obscure most of the attention directed her way.

Tommy was muttering darkly beneath his breath.

Artemis stammered, "They're not here for you," she whispered. "Or... or I don't think they are..." She trailed off, mind spinning. "I mean to say," she murmured, "I didn't call them."

"Then who are they here for?" Tommy snarled, grabbing his sister by the shoulders and shaking her.

Artemis' teeth rattled. Jamie Kramer, noticing Tommy's roughness, yelled, "Hey—stop that!"

But the others were now noticing the flashing red and blue lights. The others were starting to look up from their conversations, frowning in the direction of the windows facing the main portion of the ranch.

Forester and Wade were on their feet now, both frowning, shooting confused looks at one another but then glancing towards Artemis.

"Hey, Checkers," Forester said slowly. "You should come here for a sec."

Artemis heard voices now, outside the ranch house. She heard the sound of footsteps and boots moving up the driveway. Forester was still gesturing at her, but Wade had darted forward, pulling his ID from his pocket as he approached the door.

Forester was now moving towards her. Tommy was retreating, heading quickly out of the kitchen, down a hall and into the back of the house. The shadows of the hall swallowed her brother and that stupid leather jacket of his.

And all she could think as he left was that he hadn't answered her question.

But then, her attention was caught by a nudge at her arm.

Forester stood next to her, holding up his phone for her to see. "Know why I just got this, Checkers?"

She stared. It was an arrest warrant for her. She read the information beneath the photo of her face. She tapped her finger on the text. "What—what does that mean? The part next to code?"

"It means," Forester said grimly, "You're wanted for murder, Artemis."

And suddenly a fist was pounding on the door.

"FBI, open up!" A voice yelled.

Everyone in the house had gone still. Jamie had turned off the blaring music. Tommy had disappeared in the back.

And Artemis stood there, fear in her heart, desperately rubbing at the red stain on her sleeve.

CHAPTER TWO

WADE OPENED THE DOOR, and Artemis watched—a pit in her stomach—as the thickset FBI agent faced six other LEOs in the doorway. A combination of local PD and FBI scowled through the open threshold.

Leading the FBI, she spotted an agent she didn't recognize. A woman with pinched features—her eyes too close together, her nose too small, her lips pursed as if in ever-present disapproval. Artemis shifted uncomfortably under the scrutiny of those in the door.

A couple of the local cops tried to brush past Wade, but at the gleaming gold badge flashed in their faces, they pulled up short.

Forester gave Artemis a quick pat on the back and murmured in her ear. "You didn't kill anyone, right?"

She swallowed and opened her mouth to reply, but Forester slid past her before she could, raising a hand and greeting the figures in the door cheerfully.

"Hey Val," he said to the woman.

"Cameron," she replied, still tight-lipped.

"You look well, Val."

"Go to hell, Forester. Wade, pleasure seeing you," she said, nodding politely towards Forester's partner.

The fed in the sunglasses nodded back. "Pleasure's mine. Mind taking a second to talk?"

"Don't really see the point, Wade. You got the warrant." The woman's eyes swept the room. Then, her gaze landed on Artemis. She frowned, reaching up and brushing back her tight braids. Artemis felt glued to the spot, unsure what to do.

Tommy was long gone. Had he gone out the back?

Forester leaned in the doorway, using his lanky frame to help block access to Artemis. "Now, Val, let's be polite, kay? You know Blythe is with us."

"I see that."

"No, I mean she's with *us*. She's ra-ra-blue."

"Cameron, truly, I'm not here to spite you. I have my orders. Now please." She raised her voice, calling into the house, her narrowed eyes fixated on where Artemis lingered awkwardly. "Ms. Blythe? Please come here." The woman gestured with a hand, still standing in the threshold of the house, clearly allowing for some level of professional courtesy for the two feds blocking the way.

Artemis' sense of fear continued to speed through her. She only managed a small moment of gratitude on behalf of the two feds. Cam and Wade were standing up on her behalf. At least for now, preventing entrance into the ranch house.

Jamie was trying to interrupt, calling out. "Excuse me, what is this?"

But the agent referred to as Val ignored him. She was still gesturing towards Artemis, clicking her fingers now as if to summon her closer.

"What's the damn holdup?" A harsh voice barked out from the bottom of the stairs.

Artemis, who'd been slowly emerging from behind the counter, went still. Her heart skipped as she recognized that voice. The man belonging to that voice appeared at the base of the stairs, parting the other police by force of personality alone.

And that's when Artemis recognized the uniforms of the local cops. Jamie Kramer's ranch was near enough to the Pinelake border that it offered the perfect case study in jurisdictional dispute.

And so it was with very little surprise and very great dread that Artemis realized the brown uniforms of the Pinelake sheriff's office were in full display now.

The figure marching up the steps, with heavy footfalls, while adjusting his black belt beneath an ample belly was none other than Sergeant Larry Dawkins. She could still remember encounters in her youth with Sergeant Dawkins. Especially where Tommy was concerned—a month hadn't gone by, it had seemed, where Dawkins hadn't dragged Tommy back home after an excursion to the dam to throw rocks at the ducks or some time on a mansion's roof setting off fireworks until the police came. Tommy hadn't been a fan of the sheriff's department.

The feeling had certainly been mutual.

As for Larry Dawkins himself, back in the day he'd had darker hair and a less bushy mustache; he'd been in much better shape, and his face hadn't been nearly as red as it was now. His big, drooping, white mustache quivered in rage. This facial hair plus his prominent belly gave the man, in Artemis' psyche, the look of a walrus. His waddle and wide eyes didn't help.

The Dawkins family had always hated Artemis. In no small part because one of her father's victims had been Sheriff Dawkins' first wife. The Sergeant's own mother.

And by the look of things, for the happy task of arresting Artemis Blythe, Sergeant Dawkins had *not* come alone.

His two sons trailed behind him, both also clad in their uniforms, looking quite self-important and dapper as they climbed the steps behind their father's waddle.

Ross Dawkins was a big man with no neck. He had no hair and looked something like a boulder crossed with a brick wall. He wasn't as athletic as Forester, nor as muscled as Agent Wade. A lot of this man's size came from late night drinks after hours. Ross's brother was less imposing. A slim, reedy man with small glasses. Merl Dawkins was more bookish than his younger brother, Ross. He always had a world-weary look in his eyes.

Unlike the two other men, his attention wasn't fixated on Artemis, like some doberman eyeing a hunk of bloody meat. Instead, he glanced at his brother and father, as if making sure he didn't need to intervene and save them from themselves.

The three men came to a halt behind Val, but it was a close thing—Larry tried to bully on through, but Val held out an arm, stopping the older man. Ross tried to push the arm away, giving his father access to the house, but Forester reached out, shoving Ross's a rm.

Merl's eyes widened behind his glasses, and he took a couple of skipping steps forward, trying to place himself between his larger family members and the feds in the doorway.

"Get the hell out of my way, pirate!" snapped Ross, glaring at Forester's eye-patch. He managed to jostle past Val, sending her stumbling two steps to the side.

"Oops," Forester muttered, meeting the irate cop's gaze. "Val doesn't like being touched—ah, yup, see?"

Before the explosion of spittle from the irate man's shout could even drift, Val had stepped back in, elbow first, shoving Ross back out of the way by digging her thin, bony appendage into his bread basket. When the bald man protested, the FBI agent snapped, "Enough! Ms. Blythe, you are under arrest!"

The Washingtons gasped. Jamie was still protesting. "What for? Hey—Larry, what are you doing?"

Val continued as if she hadn't been interrupted. "For the murder of Azin Kartov."

Artemis stared at the woman, eyes the size of saucers. "I... I... *what?*"

"Don't even try," snapped the sergeant, staring murderously at her over the FBI agent's shoulder. "He had a camera, Blythe—we saw the whole thing on film."

Now, Wade even turned, glancing at her—his expression unreadable behind those sunglasses. Everyone's eyes were on her. Everyone except Forester, who was still frowning at the cops in the doorway. His back was to her, and the tall, bedraggle-haired man was saying, "Not a chance in hell. Get out of here with that."

But Val met Forester's gaze and held it. A look was passed between them, and Val said, "He's telling the truth, Forester. It's all on video."

"What's on video?" Forester snapped.

Wade had now stepped aside, moving away from the door. Artemis went cold, standing in the hall, the scent of the carrot cake and cream cheese frosting just vaguely tingeing the air.

The Dawkins brothers shouldered roughly past Forester, taking the opening Wade had allowed by stepping back. Ross reached her first, the boulder-headed man snagging her arm and twisting it hard.

"Hey!" Jamie yelled. "Cut that out! Ross! Cut it out!"

Artemis gasped in pain as her arm moved up behind her back. Wade watched, inscrutable, his dark glasses reflecting ribbons of light from the balloon tails.

Forester turned sharply, pointing a finger at Ross and Merl, who were cuffing Artemis none-too-gently. "Hey, ugly—I'll rearrange that stupid nose if you keep twisting her wrist like that!"

"Forester!" Val snapped.

"Agent?" Forester retorted, still keeping his eye on Ross, who was snapping cuffs in place.

The metal bit into Artemis' wrist, and then he tightened further, eliciting a gasp of pain. But Artemis tried to keep it under her breath. She didn't want Forester to fly off the handle on account of her.

Jamie was still protesting. The Washingtons were watching, aghast, but Cynthia had pulled her phone out, videoing. "Don't worry Artemis!" the woman exclaimed. "I have it all on video!"

Artemis just winced, not wanting to glance back in the analyst's direction.

"Forester... Calm down, Cam," Val was saying. "It's on camera. It's all on camera. Please—don't get yourself in trouble over this."

Forester snapped, "What is on camera? You still didn't say!"

"The murder! Artemis Blythe shot a man in the chest twice. We have it on video. Now *move*!" Val used a similar trick with her elbow to clear Forester out of her way now. She reached Artemis' side, deftly taking her by the shoulder and tugging insistently, leading her away from the Dawkins brothers.

"We've cleared a room back at Pinelake," Sergeant Larry Dawkins said quickly, smoothing his mustache. "You can use our facilities."

"That's fine," Val said, tight-lipped.

Jamie yelled, "Don't take her *there*! They'll kill her!"

"Shut up and eat your cake, Jamie," Ross retorted. Merl just moved after his brother, trying to usher the bigger man back towards the door.

Artemis, in a daze, was led out of the house full of the people she cared most about in the world, her hands behind her back, cuffs locked tight. Her heart pounded horribly, and all she could think of was her meeting with Azin.

She'd spoken with him less than an hour ago...

She hadn't known things would turn out the way they had.

And if she'd known *this* was coming, she never would have gone to Azin's oceanside residence to begin with.

As Val escorted Artemis towards a waiting car, the Dawkins family members hastened to their own vehicle, hurrying to hop in and preparing to escort Artemis back to their grandfather's police station.

Azin was dead... *dead...* Artemis let out a gasping breath. But Azin's life wasn't the only one jeopardized. If she went to the Pinelake sheriff's department... The Dawkins had had it out for Artemis for years now. If she was going to be held at their police station...

She shivered.

The chances of making it out alive were slim to none.

Chapter Three

A television was wheeled into the cold, concrete room. An old, tube tv that looked like it might topple and crash at any moment. Val, who'd given her name as "Agent Butcher" to Artemis, was busily fiddling with a couple of red and yellow wires leading from a black box to the back of the ancient television. The woman in the charcoal suit bent, pursing her already tight lips to blow. A sheet of dust erupted off the back of the television, and Agent Butcher straightened, glancing back across the interrogation room table.

Artemis fidgeted uncomfortably. The tight cuffs continued to bite into her wrists, and she winced in pain every time she shifted. This was all a mistake. It had to be. She already rehearsed how things had gone with Azin... It didn't make sense. Why did they think she'd done this? She could feel herself starting to hyperventilate but attempted one of the breathing tricks one of her many shrinks had tried to instill. It helped. Barely.

Her eyes darted to the closed door of the bare room. Twice, already, the door had opened and closed, for no other reason than to allow passing gawkers to get a good look at the "Ghost-killer's daughter" finally getting her due comeuppance.

The only other policeman allowed in the room had been Sergeant Dawkins. The walrus-shaped man sat with his arms folded over his belly, glaring at Artemis, and occasionally shooting impatient looks towards where Butcher prepped the television.

Forester and Wade had said they'd follow her to the Pinelake station, but she had yet to see hide nor hair of either. Nearly half an hour had passed since the fateful party. She hadn't heard from anyone.

She didn't doubt that the Dawkins and their fellow officers in the sheriff's department were playing interference while Artemis was under their supervision.

The moment she was most dreading, though, was when the FBI agents left for their hotels or motels, leaving her in some dark, solitary cell with no one for company save members of a sheriff's department who loathed her family's name.

But another moment of dread was now about to play out in front of her.

Artemis stared at the television screen, nervous, feeling her skin prickle. She shifted in her seat, glancing towards Butcher.

The FBI agent had finally brought up whatever video file she'd intended. Artemis spotted white lettering in the bottom right corner.

Two big white lines down the center of the otherwise dark screen suggested the video was currently paused.

Agent Butcher turned to Artemis, her narrow eyes set in a cold face. Her dark braids had small, red beads in them, shifting under the naked bulb in the ceiling as she regarded Artemis.

"Do you know what I'm about to show you?"

"No."

"This video was taken from about an hour ago."

"Yes."

"May I ask, Ms. Blythe, where you were an hour ago?"

Artemis hesitated, swallowed. No sense in lying. "At Azin's place."

Butcher's thin eyebrows moved up ever so slightly but course corrected and settled. "I presume you mean Azin Kartov?"

Artemis face felt numb. She nodded. "Yes."

"She admits it!" Sergeant Dawkins exclaimed, pounding a flat hand against the table. "Like father like daughter—you heard her!"

"Please, sir," said Val sharply, turning. "Let me conduct the interview. You are here as a courtesy to your department. Don't make me ask you to leave."

"I'd like to see your bony ass try," muttered the large cop, but he eventually settled with a petulant wiggle of his wide hips. His red-face turned to Artemis', reminding her of Mars.

She tried not to meet his gaze.

Agent Butcher returned her attention to her suspect. "Before we watch this, why don't you tell me, in your words, what happened?"

"Umm... Okay." Artemis paused, frowning. She closed her eyes for a moment, pulling up the memories. She had often been able to file away experiences for later recollection. She didn't think of her memory as photographic, but there were aspects that could be described as such.

She played the memory forward. Remembered stepping out of the taxi. The scent of the salt on the wind. The crash of ocean waves against the shore, only a few hundred feet away from the front door. She remembered approaching the door, pressing the buzzer.

And then...

She murmured, "I arrived at his place. I buzzed."

"Then?" Butcher said.

"He let me in... wait, no. The door was already open."

"Did Mr. Kartov say anything?"

Artemis closed her eyes again, then nodded. She echoed the memory, " *Door is open—just push!*" her eyes opened again.

"Then what happened?"

"Then... then I entered the house. He smiled and nodded. I approached."

"Then what?"

"I was there to study chess openings."

"And did you?"

"No!"

"Why not?"

"Because we didn't get to it."

"Why not?" Butcher said insistently, wielding her words like a hammer against rock, slowly but surely bludgeoning it to pieces.

Artemis considered this, shaking her head.

"Let's slow down," Butcher said. "What happened next?"

"Well... He said something to me."

"Do you remember what? Try to get the phrasing right."

"I remember exactly what he said." Artemis wrinkled her nose. "*As beautiful as you look in your profile picture. A pleasure to meet again.*"

"That's what he said?"

"That's it?"

"She's admitting it," said Dawkins, muttering now and nodding, wagging his red face so that his double chin squished. "She's admitting the whole thing!" He looked back and up, noticing the blinking red camera and giving a happy little wave. The sergeant turned back around, making a shooing gesture as if to say *get on with it.*

Butcher was glaring now. Artemis frowned at the camera. She hadn't seen any camera at Azin's place, but she hadn't been looking for one. She knew Kartov had always been a bit paranoid. She also remembered he *had* shown her a camera *outside* the house. Is that what they'd meant?

"Then what happened?" said the agent.

"Then... Well, I greeted him."

"What did you say?"

"Hello, Azin. Hopefully I didn't startle you by ringing the bell." Then, before Butcher could press further, Artemis continued this strange play-by-play. It wasn't like she had anything to hide. Especially if it was all on camera. What she couldn't understand, of course, was why on earth they thought she'd killed the man.

Still, she continued, slowly, "He said, *no, no, not at all. I recognized you on the camera. See?* He then pointed towards a video screen by the door. He continued, *I knew you were coming, though, so I left the front door open."* Artemis hesitated, frowning. This part was cloudy for a moment, but she pieced together the sounds, the thoughts, the memories then pressed on. "I said, *When was our last meeting? Two months ago, right? It's been a while.*"

Butcher spoke now, cutting Artemis off, "And he replied, *two months ago, yes. Seattle Open. You beat me quite handily with black. Though five months before that, a draw, remember?*"

Artemis stared at the agent now. She frowned. "H-how did you know that?" then she answered her question. "It's on camera?"

"It's all on camera, girl!" Dawkins yelled, rocking back in his chair and nodding rapidly. "We've got you. By God, we've *got* you this time!"

Artemis stared at the screen. Agent Butcher seemed to have decided it was the time to show the movie. She pressed something on the black box, and the picture began to move.

A clear, high-definition image, suggesting it had been recorded by advanced equipment. The image started by showing Azin Kartov, sitting on a red chair, leaning back and sipping wine. He swirled the wine.

And then things proceeded exactly as Artemis remembered. Exactly as she'd just told Agent Butcher and Sergeant Dawkins.

She watched, frowning faintly in polite confusion.

"Is this you?" asked Agent Butcher said, pointing.

A new figure had appeared on the screen. There she stood, wearing the same red sweater with the white snowflakes that Artemis was currently sitting in. The same short-cut, dark hair. The woman's face flashed by the camera, revealing two mismatched eyes.

Artemis stared at an image of herself as the figure came to a stop in the middle of the room. Just as she'd remembered doing.

Azin was speaking. *"As beautiful as you look in your profile picture. A pleasure to meet again."*

Exactly as she remembered. It played out before her eyes. She was still frowning quizzically. She knew how the scene ended. So what did they think she'd done?

"Hello, Azin. Hopefully I didn't startle you by ringing the bell," Artemis replied in the video.

They went back and forth, playing the scene out exactly, word for word, as Artemis remembered. Azin swirled his wineglass a second time, smiling now. Clearly attempting to be charming but failing.

Artemis said, *"When was our last meeting? Two months ago, right? It's been a while."*

Azin replied in the way Butcher had narrated. Not a word out of place. Every movement, how Artemis had remembered. She found herself somewhat distracted by the predatory leer of Sergeant Dawkins across the table.

But more importantly, she found herself distracted by the movie itself.

"I don't understand," Artemis said slowly. "What am I supposed to be seeing? I told you—*I did see him.* This doesn't mean I hurt him. I visited him an hour ago... If he's dead, someone else did it!"

But Butcher just pointed a finger at the screen as it continued. Again, exactly as Artemis remembered.

She laughed. "If I remember correctly, you started trading pieces by move three."

"Hmm, oh well," he said. "Strategies take time to arrange, don't they?"

"Yes. Well, should we get to it? I don't want to be up too late. Some of my friends are throwing a party for me at my friend's ranch." She shrugged sheepishly. "I told them I'd be a bit tardy, though."

"Of course, of course. My book of openings. I had three of them marked," Azin said, pointing down. He briefly lowered his eyes, as well as his glass of wine.

And then things shifted.

Artemis went still in the interrogation room chair, freezing in place. "Wait," she said sharply. "No—no, hang on. That's not right."

It was like watching a nightmare unfold. Everything like the memory as she recalled it. The woman hadn't moved from where she'd come to stand still. The red sweater, the white snowflakes, the dark hair, the occasional glimpse of a mismatched eye since Artemis stood with her profile displayed to the camera. Even the occasional tap of fingers against her hip how Artemis so often did when nervous or uncomfortable.

It was as she tapped her fingers and shifted uncomfortably that the memory changed.

If she hadn't been watching for herself, she would have thought some-one was playing a joke.

"It's been altered!" Artemis said. "That—right there—I never did that!"

"Altered, *please*!" Dawkins snorted.

Butcher had frozen the scene where Artemis was reaching towards her waistband, moving the red sweater aside.

Butcher frowned at Artemis. "Altered how?"

"I never did that!" Artemis exclaimed, shaking her head. Now, though, the Artemis in the movie was moving her fingers towards her waist, Artemis didn't want to see what came next. The gesture was a small one, innocuous. Except it *wasn't* what had happened. Which meant something was wrong. "The footage!" Artemis snapped. "Someone altered the footage!"

"It was taken directly from his cloud server," Butcher shot back. "No alterations at all. We had to contact the security company directly just to get the file. This is raw footage, Artemis. Are you saying you blacked out? You don't remember what you did?"

"What I did? What did I do?"

In response, Butcher clicked the box again. And the horrible, mind-bending video continued to play.

"Azin?" Something had changed in her voice. "Azin?" she said, louder. "One other thing…"

Kartov looked up. He went still.

"Artemis?" he said slowly, staring at the woman. "Ms. Blythe," he said, louder. "Wait—hey, hey!"

A gun was pointed at his head. She stood there, her posture one of complete defiance., her pale features visible from the side, one blue eye narrowed. "You knew this was coming, Azin," she murmured. "You had to know."

And then she pulled the trigger twice.

Two loud bangs!

Azin shot back, nearly tilting the red chair. It rocked on its heels from the momentum, then hit the ground again with a thud. He stared down, mouth open. He gaped at his chest, looked up, terror in his eyes. He looked down again, uttering a single strangled syllable. "Why?"

Two streams of blood burbled over his heart, pouring down his chest, along his stomach. He shifted once more, taking a shaking, hesitant breath. But his throat rasped as if the air had lodged somewhere.

He let out a final groan and then his eyes fluttered, closing tight.

Artemis Blythe stood over him, gun still in her hand, wearing her red sweater with small white snowflakes stitched along the hems. She watched as crimson poured down his chest and dribbled onto the floor. Then she whispered. "Sorry, Azin. But... one enemy at a time."

Then Artemis turned to leave, her face flashing across the camera once more. The same mis-matched eyes. The same pale, pretty features. The same dark hair.

"Wait, hang on—that's not clear enough. That's not me... that... that can't be me!" Artemis yelled. Butcher paused the video, pointing. The footage wasn't as clear due to the motion. Artemis' hair whipped about her face.

Dawkins was chortling. "Same demon eyes. Same face. Same hair. Same sweater. Ha! It's her. It's absolutely her! We've caught you this time, Blythe!"

Butcher didn't cut him off but instead watched Artemis as if gauging the woman's reaction.

Artemis didn't know what to say. She stared at the movie on the screen, certain she was in a dream.

No... no, a nightmare.

This couldn't be happening. How could this be happening? Everything had started out exactly how she remembered. But that last part, the gun, the gunshots. That's not how it had happened at all.

But if the video footage wasn't edited, if the security company itself had given raw footage, then how was that possible? Unless Agent Butcher was lying?

But why would she? What did she have to gain?

Artemis was shaking her head, feeling as if something was short-circuiting in her mind. She hesitated, murmuring to herself, trying to make sense of everything. She said, slowly, "There's been a mistake."

"No mistake!" Dawkins exclaimed.

"We found the gun, Ms. Blythe," Butcher said, quietly. She pressed a button on the black box, and the file name in the bottom right changed. This time, the image showed Artemis leaving the house, pausing and then throwing something over the rail into the bushes.

Butcher stepped behind the television and emerged with the plastic evidence bag, which she held up to the light. "It has your fingerprints on it, Artemis. Two bullets fired. The gun is registered in your name."

Artemis stared, stammering. "That's not mine."

"Are you saying you didn't throw this into the bushes? Do we need to replay the video?"

"I threw something, but it wasn't that! I've never seen that in my life. I don't own a gun."

"So what are you throwing in this image?"

The video footage shifted back. And again, it showed Artemis, clearly distraught, hurrying down the steps and tossing something over the rail. Butcher paused the video this time. She said, firmly, "is this clear enough an image of you?"

Most of the video up to this point had been from the side, or brief flashes of movement. But now, all plausible deniability vanished.

The high-definition, outdoor camera caught Artemis leaving, taking the steps two at a time. There was still blur, her hair still shifted about her face. Until the very end. She reached the sidewalk, rubbed her hand off on her hip, and then looked up, directly at the camera.

Butcher froze the image. "Artemis Blythe, is that you?"

Artemis stared at the image, mouth unhinged. It wasn't a trick of the light. It wasn't a look-alike. It wasn't some man in a wig. It was her. It was the face she stared at in the mirror. Artemis stared at herself, stared at a woman fleeing a murder scene having just discarded the murder weapon.

And yet she couldn't remember any of that. "That's me," Artemis said, her voice small. "But I didn't kill him. That's not what happened."

"Then who is this?" said the woman, pointing at the screen.

All sorts of wild ideas and theories went through Artemis' mind. Partly, she wondered if someone had perfect plastic surgery, sculpting their face to look like hers. She immediately discarded this thought. People who underwent plastic surgery had a rigidness about their expressions, but the look of fear in the eyes of the woman on the video was all too apparent. Another, even wilder theory wondered if maybe Helen had survived after all, and maybe this was her sister. The only reason she had even thought this, though, was because the person in the video looked so much like her. It was her. It was exactly her.

But Helen had never looked like Artemis. She had been prettier, with Bambi eyes, sharper cheekbones, and an upturned, celestial nose that had always made Artemis jealous. Helen had curled hair and was quite a bit taller than Artemis.

No, this wasn't some long lost sister pretending. It wasn't some doppelgänger or plastic surgery recipient. The woman staring at the camera, fear in her eyes, having just discarded something into the bushes was Artemis.

Artemis could remember casting the item in the bush, could remember reaching the bottom of the stairs, could even remember looking up and spotting the camera.

But she hadn't killed anyone. She hadn't thrown away a gun.

These far-fetched theories only further bothered her. She didn't even know if Helen was alive, and if so, her sister had been compassionate, kind, strong. She wasn't a murderer. Briefly, Artemis remembered the question she had asked Tommy. A question he had refused to answer.

Which reminded her that she did have a twin. But not identical.

It was testament to just how mind bending the video was that Artemis struggled desperately to figure out what she was seeing. She felt as if she was going insane.

She stammered, shook her head, and said, "that's not what happened." It wasn't very useful, but she kept repeating it. "That isn't what happened."

"Would you like me to play it again?" said Butcher. "Maybe it will jog your memory?"

Artemis didn't say anything, just sat there, numb. Butcher began to play the video once more. And again, the movie played exactly as Artemis remembered. She had been there. She had said those things. She had walked into the room; she had greeted the man. They had exchanged pleasantries, mild teasing about their previous meetings. He had greeted her, clearly recognizing who she was.

Butcher was clearly good at her job, because she paused the video at this very part. She played it again. Azin said to the dark-haired woman, who stood with her side facing the camera, *"I recognized you on the camera."*

Butcher looked up. "Azin sure seemed to recognize you," Butcher said quietly. "He mentions how beautiful you are later. You remember that comment?"

"I... I do." Artemis just stared. Her head was starting to hurt.

Butcher's point was clear. Artemis recognized herself. Especially leaving the apartment. Artemis remembered everything up to a point, proving she'd been there. Azin recognized her as well; they'd met twice before in tournaments and, like a lot of opponents, he'd probably studied many of her online matches.

Which left Artemis with a horrible dilemma.

She *knew* she hadn't killed Azin.

But the video footage from the security cameras said otherwise. And that's when Dawkins suddenly said. "Look—look on her sweater, there!"

Butcher looked down. So did Artemis.

She was still wearing the red sweater with white snowflakes which Sophie Kramer had given her. Dawkins was pointing at the sleeve, towards the stain of cocktail sauce Jamie had noticed. Butcher frowned at the sleeve.

"It's blood!" Dawkins exclaimed. "I bet you it's *his* blood." A pudgy finger pointed at the television screen. The man was on his feet now, huffing from the effort of standing. He waved that finger about like a conductor's baton. "We have video of the murder. She admitted herself she was there. She practically recited the meeting from memory! She identified herself. She's seen throwing the gun away, and the weapon was found with *her* fingerprints, registered in *her* name." Then, the finger jammed towards the sleeve in a final, devastating flourish. "And that is blood!"

"No... no, it's cocktail sauce," Artemis said quietly.

But even as she mentioned it... she wasn't sure she believed it. As she stared at her sleeve, she realized the stain was a bit *too* dark to be sauce. In addition, she had never been anywhere near the shrimp platter.

It couldn't be blood... could it?

Artemis looked up. Butcher was pulling a handcuff key from her belt. "I'm going to need that sweater, Ms. Blythe. Please stand up."

Artemis complied, numb. What else could she do?

"That's not what happened," she repeated again, feeling like a broken record stuck on repeat. "Azin didn't... it wasn't..." She trailed off, lips buzzing, mind reeling.

The key slipped into the cuffs. They were removed. The sweater followed.

Artemis stood in a thin t-shirt, shivering in the cold interrogation room. Sergeant Dawkins' hateful gaze pierced her, like a pin through a butterfly.

"We've got you now," he murmured. "We've got you."

Chapter Four

Artemis sat in the prison cell, her mind reeling. The cold bars pressed against her spine as she leaned back on the metal cot. No blankets. No pillow. She hadn't had water in two hours. No food, either—she hadn't had a chance to eat anything at the party before the cops had shown up.

Another red light watched her from the police station's hall ceiling.

Artemis stared at the camera. She blinked. It didn't.

The door suddenly buzzed. She stiffened, jolting with terror. She turned sharply, tense on the cot, staring towards the open door at the end of the hall. That little red light watching her was the only protection she had.

If that ever went off... Ross Dawkins or his father... or even the grandfather, Abraham Dawkins, the sheriff, would likely be standing outside the bars.

Of all of them, the one she was most scared of was the boulder-headed Ross. He didn't just *hate* her. He was also something of a sadist in a uniform. There was no telling what he might do in the dark, in a cell, with no one around to stop him.

Another prickle of fear dabbed down Artemis' spine. But as she turned on the cold metal cot, facing the door, she felt a sudden flicker of relief.

It was somewhat short-lived though.

Agent Forester was moving towards her, his long strides eating up the hall in quick fashion. He came to a halt outside her door, peering in. "Well," he said slowly. "You look like shit."

"Cameron. I didn't do this."

"Hmm. You sure?"

"Yes!"

"I had to hand over my gun to come back here. Guess they didn't trust me. Don't think that lumpy one likes me much."

"Ross? No—he hates anyone who..." She trailed off. She'd been about to say *who likes me.* But she wasn't sure if this was the case. She didn't know what Wade or Forester thought about her now. No doubt, Supervising Agent Grant was already calling in the termination papers.

Artemis Blythe would end up being the FBI's shortest-term consultant ever.

Forester leaned against the bars, peering at her, his calloused hands poking through, tapping the inside. "They've got video," he said.

"I know."

"I saw it."

"You did? Shit." Artemis winced.

"Looks bad," he replied.

"I... I know." She swallowed, shaking her head. "I don't know how... I... I mean... It's gotta be connected to my Dad, right? Or... or my background? I don't know. It makes no sense."

"Look, Checkers," Forester said quietly, "It doesn't look good for you. They found blood on your sweater."

Artemis' stomach sank. This had been the one thing she'd been hoping for. She'd been confident there hadn't been blood on her sweater. How could there have been? She *hadn't* shot Azin.

"It's his blood," Forester said. "Quick match—they'll have the lab double check. But it's the murder victim's blood. Azin's body is at the coroner's now. They already signed off that you shot him with your gun."

"That's not my gun!"

"It's registered in your name."

"Registered *where*?"

"Town of Welsford," Forester said simply. "Isn't that where Grant set you up?"

Artemis just stared. She'd been living in the rental Grant had gotten for her for nearly a month now. Living in Welsford. She hadn't even known Welsford *had* a gun store *to* register at.

"Your prints are on the gun."

"I heard, I heard! It's not possible."

"Video of you throwing it into a bush."

She yelled, "I didn't do that!"

Forester just watched her, tilting his head. "Never took you for a liar."

"I'm not!"

"No," Forester said. A streak of moonlight caught his handsome features, coming from the window in her cell and spotlighting the tall man. "I'm not saying you are. I'm saying you ain't. What did you throw in that bush?"

Artemis just huffed. "I threw a tube of newspaper clippings into the bushes. That's all!"

"What?"

"Newspaper clippings. Azin gave me some newspaper clippings and old photos. They were of my father—tracking the Ghost-killer's murders. Azin was very interested in all of it. I left early because I was upset. Very upset. Azin seemed to think I shouldn't be allowed at the tournament because of..." She swallowed. "Because of my past. He said he was going to report me to the officials. To get me kicked out. So I left. I stopped to throw that damn tube of clippings *while* leaving. That's it. Not a gun. A tube."

Forester studied her in the dark, nodding slowly. "Artemis," he murmured.

"What?" she demanded, exasperated.

"Whatever you do, don't tell Val about that."

"About what?"

"That camera behind us. No audio. Understand? So speak quietly on this."

"On what part?"

"What you just said about Azin wanting to turn you in to the tournament officials, to get you kicked out. *That*," he said firmly, his lips drawn into a thin line, "is what us pros like to call *motive*. Ever heard of it?"

"Don't be flippant!" she snapped.

"I'm not. I'm telling you, Val is a by the book type of gal. She is going to cross every T and dot every I and figure out how to make sure when she hands this off to the DA, it's packaged in a nice little parcel with a big, double-loop bow. Got me? Any judge worth their salt at this point would happily chuck a library at you. If you give them *motive* along with... you know, *everything else,* then you're going down. Hard. That clear?"

Artemis was finding it difficult to breathe now. She tried to nod but was beginning to hyperventilate and leaned back in her cell again, her shoulders trying to find some comfort against the rigid metal bars. "Dear God," she murmured. "I'm done. I'm *done.*"

"Hang on, now," Forester cut in. "No sense getting dramatic." He pushed away from the bars, crossing his arms and frowning at her. With her sitting, it only further emphasized the height difference between the two of them. He sucked air slowly, clicking his teeth. The scar on the inside of his hand flashed. The man shook his head, shot a look back towards the open door. "Technically, I've only got about a minute left. So you need to tell me *everything.* What happened at Azin's?"

Artemis paused, trying to think clearly. It was hard to do with such loud thoughts raging in her mind. Also somewhat hard with such a loud Hawaiian shirt on the other side of the bars. Forester studied her close though, his dark eyes narrowed.

"I... It's exactly as the video shows. Up until—"

"The incriminating part."

"Yes!"

"That sounds convenient."

"I know!" she yelled, slapping her hands petulantly against the seat on either side of her and instantly wincing and wishing she hadn't. "I sat down with Azin. We opened his chess manual. We started an opening and then he asked me about my father. He looked upset. Troubled. He mentioned that he didn't think a killer's daughter should have influence. Didn't think I should have a platform. Said he was going to quit the tournament if I didn't. Said he was going to bring it to the officials. He then handed me the news clippings. Like some sort of proof. I stormed out. That's all."

"You didn't shoot him."

"I told you I didn't."

"But the video—"

"I know..." she said, exhausted now, slumping in her seat. "The footage has to be doctored."

"It isn't," Cameron said. "Checked it myself. Raw footage. Wade checked it—he's a nerd. Agrees. No one changed the footage."

She whined, "How's that possible?"

Forester studied her. "I can think of one way..."

"I didn't kill him," she murmured, the strength leaving her in a faint whimper. She wanted to curl up, to lie down and go to sleep.

Forester adjusted his eye patch, swallowing once. For a brief moment, as he watched her tremble in the cell, the moonlight streaking his features, he looked... *different.* Gentler somehow. There was something in his eyes... something fierce.

She'd seen it before. But couldn't quite remember when. It was all too much to keep track of.

Vaguely, she seemed to recall Forester saying she reminded him of someone. But who? She couldn't say.

"You helped me instead of going after the bad guy," Forester said simply. "I owe you one."

An image of sprinting for cups of water to help flush the fed's eyes flashed through Artemis' mind. She just shrugged.

"I can't say I believe you, Artemis," Forester said simply. "I mean... I do, and I don't. I know you sometimes have panic attacks. Do you... you know... ever black out?"

"No! No, I don't. I'm not insane, Cameron!"

Forester began to reply, but a voice suddenly shouted down the hall. "Hey—enough! Time's up. Cell's closing for visitors for the night. You can jaw tomorrow!"

Forester held up a finger towards the open door. "One minute!" he called.

"No minutes. Hurry up, boss's orders!"

Forester did not hurry up. Instead, he said to Artemis, "I'll do what I can. But... I'm not sure how I can help, Checkers. I really don't know. I mean... If the guy had it coming, maybe I could understand why—"

"I didn't *kill him!*"

Forester's hands shot up as if in surrender. He adjusted his eye patch, shrugged and then turned. Whistling, he slowly strolled away, taking his sweet time about it, if only to infuriate the cop in the doorway.

Artemis didn't watch. Her head found her hands hanging low, and her stomach continued to flip and twist in knots.

Fingerprints on a gun she didn't buy. Blood on her sweater. Video footage of the murder.

Had she blacked out?

Was she... was she going insane?

Was this how her father had felt when it had started? Maybe... maybe her old man hadn't been in control. Maybe the first time he'd killed, it had been something like this. A memory he didn't know he had. A memory buried, rebelled against.

"I'm going insane..." she murmured, quiet enough so only she could hear.

She was just so damn tired. She leaned back, head resting slowly against the cold metal surface of the cot. No blanket, no pillow, just darkness and frigidity.

Had she actually killed Azin?

If so, why couldn't she remember?

She closed her eyes, trying to block out the intrusive thoughts. The door in the hallway clanged shut, sealing her off from the outside world.

From freedom.

Would she ever taste the open air again?

Or was her freedom gone forever?

Worse... had she murdered an innocent man without even knowing?

The tightness in her stomach only intensified, growing worse. And that's when the panic attack came, rushing through her system like a freight train.

CHAPTER FIVE

A FAINT *CLICK*. AND Artemis' head jolted off the cot. Her skin prick-led and tremors crept up her arms and legs. She winced at a crick in her neck from having slept awkwardly on a bent arm in lieu of a pillow. No blanket, and so the tremors accompanied shivers.

But the fear at the sudden sound soon displaced any sense of discom-fort. Artemis peered through the bars in the direction of the opening door. She stared, her heart pounding wildly.

The cells on either side of her remained empty, and she stared in the direction of the entrance to the long hall.

The door was propped open. She heard voices, whispers. A figure shifted, his shadow cast by the light along the ground. She felt a slow trickle of terror as she recognized the voice of Ross Dawkins.

She thought she caught a brief glimpse, through the bars, of the pale, bald man standing in the doorway, whispering to a smaller, slimmer figure. Artemis' heart hammered, and her eyes darted to the camera outside her cell.

The small red light was no longer blinking.

The dead camera lens stared at her with a dark, reflective gaze, and horror welled within her.

"You sure?" a voice was whispering from the open door. "She's sleeping. Let's do it now!"

Artemis didn't move, she just stared, her eyes gaping in the dark, her senses returning rapidly. Memories of the previous night, of the horrible events, all came flooding back. Her one small hand bunched in a fist at her side, and she felt a horrible shiver along her spine.

Should she yell? Try to startle them? Or would the shouting only irritate them. They'd turned off the camera, which meant whatever they had in store for her was not going to be pleasant.

The two shadowy figures in the hallway door lingered a moment longer.

But then, they paused.

Artemis did too, her heart full of fear.

"Hear that?" one of the voices whispered, it sounded like Merl Dawkins, the bespectacled, older brother.

"Don't lose your nerve now," snapped Ross.

"No—hush. I heard something."

Artemis had too. A scraping sound followed by a whir. She hesitated. And then, suddenly, there was a loud *smash!* In the distance, an alarm started blaring.

"Shit!" Ross said. "What was that?"

"Dunno—go, go see what—"

But Merl's response was cut off as the door slammed shut and the two brothers beat a hasty retreat to go investigate the source of the sudden sound.

All the while, Artemis sat on the metal cot, trembling. Her mind filled with horrible images of what the Dawkins brothers had intended. In their minds, her father had killed their grandmother. Whatever they did to some low-life killer was justified. Artemis wasn't sure they intended for her to see morning.

She cursed beneath her breath, rose to her feet and approaching the bars. She rattled them, hard. But the metal was solid. She checked the lock. Secured.

She held back a desire to shout in frustration, shaking the bars some more. All this accomplished was sending a buzzing sensation through her fingers. She slumped back now, leaning against the bars and feeling a sudden, unbidden lump in her throat.

Artemis leaned against the cold metal, eyes closed. She wanted to sob. Wanted to cry, but tears were as elusive to her as they had been for nearly fifteen years.

Her emotions often gathered in her gut in the form of panic. And now, she could feel her stomach tightening, could feel the fear rising within her. She took a shaky breath, fists clenched, trying to breathe properly. How many shrinks had she seen over the years? Counselors, psychologists, psychiatrists... a virtual parade of professionals.

But none of them had been able to help. Most folks with higher education liked being the smartest person in the room, and so when Artemis asked questions or questioned solutions, they'd often suggested she was simply unteachable.

Then again, perhaps some of the blame landed squarely on her shoulders.

Artemis massaged the bridge of her nose, inhaling deeply, holding the breath, then exhaling. Like this, she attempted—desperately—to steady herself. She closed her eyes, trying to count to seven as she inhaled. Then she exhaled for eight seconds.

The trick was to exhale longer than inhaling.

Like this, she managed to control the growing knot in her stomach. But of what use was that? The Dawkins would be back soon enough. They would return to her cell, in the dark, and without anyone looking, they would—

"Psst!"

She froze and glanced around.

"Psst! Hey! Art?"

She turned, looking through the cells, frowning. "H-hello?"

"Art, get back from the wall!"

"T-tommy..." She stammered simply out of disbelief. "Is that *you*?"

"Yeah. Now get back from the wall!"

Artemis turned now, realizing the voice was coming through the bars of the window above her cot. The glass had been closed the last time she'd looked. There was no way to manipulate it from the inside. But now, the window was cracked. Quite literally. Someone had smashed a corner of it.

But that hadn't been the sound she'd heard. The sound that had redirected the Dawkins' brothers had been far, far louder.

"Tommy?" she said, whispering at the cracked window. "What are you doing?"

"Back from the wall, sis. I mean it."

Artemis was already on the other side of the cell, leaning against metal bars. She swallowed hesitantly. "Umm... Tommy. Don't do anything—"

And that's when five tons of truck barreled straight into the opposite wall, the large, black battering ram of a grill smashing through cinderblock. Bits of stone and cement went flying, scattering across the ground, raining rubble inside the cell. Dust fluttered around her and settled on most available surfaces.

Small flecks of stone skipped over Artemis' cheeks, and she winced against the assault. A *larger* piece of rock—nearly the size of her head—slammed into the bars with a resounding *clang* only inches from her skull.

Angry headlights glared through the black grill of the large truck. The horn was blaring now, and Artemis glimpsed a figure gesticulating wildly from inside the truck, behind the windshield. Because of the dust, the ringing in her ears, the shock of the moment, Artemis struggled to discern much about the figure waving at her.

But Tommy's voice yelled over the blaring horn and the ringing. "Hey, sis! When I back up, run through—meet me behind the truck! Got it?"

Artemis just stared, absolutely stunned.

The door to the cell block slammed open, and loud voices bellowed through. She turned, cursed, and spotted where Ross and Merl were now sprinting towards her. Ross's eyes looked like those of an incensed pit bull. His gun was in his hand. He was aiming towards her.

"She's running!" he screamed.

Artemis dove in time. A loud *bang*! A bullet skimmed off the metal bar behind her, casting sparks. The blaring horn of the truck continued to pulsate in odd rhythms. The large vehicle growled in exertion, and then it began to move, pulling back through the opening, dislodging more stone and sending sheets of dust tumbling, along with the entire window fixture which smashed on the ground.

Artemis didn't hesitate though.

Lingering wasn't an option.

Tommy had really done it now. She cursed, sprinting forward. She thought she heard another gunshot. But the pain in her foot wasn't from a bullet but rather from where she nearly tripped over the fallen window frame.

She followed the black grill of the—undoubtedly stolen—truck back out into the parking lot.

As she tasted fresh air, her heart soared, but she was still too disoriented to fully focus on what was happening. She raced around the side of the truck, panting heavily.

Ross and Merl were now in the cell, having opened the lock. Ross was screaming after her, raising his gun again.

"Tommy?" Artemis yelled.

No sign of her brother. Where the hell had he gone?

She was behind the large truck, outside the smashed wall of the police station. Sirens were wailing now. She could hear loud voices shouting from around the building as well as from within her cell.

Then, there was a sudden *thump*. And the back door to the hauling truck was kicked open. The metal door scraped as it widened, and a figure sat inside, astride a motorbike.

Tommy gunned the engine. Artemis yelped.

Merl and Ross emerged from the cell, and Ross took a third shot.

Artemis flung herself forward. The bullet skimmed off the ground, and Tommy—the engine of his bike growling—swooped down the ramp of the truck; hit the ground, leaving a streak of black rubber, and then snared Artemis around the waist, tossing her onto the back of his vehicle.

"Hang on!" he yelled, which had been her plan to begin with.

She gripped her brother's shoulders tightly. Tommy let out a sudden shout of exhilaration as he twisted the handle, and they sped away through a smashed section of metal fence.

Tommy paused long enough to adjust the radio fixture on his console. Loud, heavy music began to blare—all electric guitars and thundering drums.

Tommy, who wasn't wearing a helmet, began to bob his head in time with the music. His long, wild hair whipped about behind him as he sped away from the scene of the crime, breaking every speed limit available.

Sirens wailed behind them, but Tommy was already moving through an alley, moving between two rows of buildings and then hastening in the direction of Pinelake's namesake. Wilderness routes around the lake, through the deep woods, were far harder to traverse without an ATV or some off-road motorbike.

Tommy knew this area like the back of his hand, though.

And the faster they cut through the night—Artemis' heart in her throat, her pulse pounding wild—the further they escaped from any pursuit. All the while, the heavy metal blared from Tommy's radio, and Artemis held on for dear life.

CHAPTER SIX

ARTEMIS' HAND PRESSED AGAINST the splintered wood where she stood in the doorway, wrinkling her nose. The scent of mold hung heavy on the stale air inside the small shed. She glanced back at where Tommy was tossing his driving gloves onto the back seat of the bike.

The shed was built into the side of a cliff, and Artemis could hear the sound of water splashing against the red stone at the base of the cliff.

"What is this place?" she said.

Tommy regarded her, frowning. "You don't remember?"

"It looks familiar."

"Used to be a lot more trees. They've changed. Ice fishing."

She hesitated, and then her eyes widened. She turned away from the moldy shed, frowning. "Why are we here?"

He looked up at her. "Ross was going to crack your skull. I came by to stop that. You're welcome."

"Thank you."

"Yeah, well, after I heard what they wanted, I couldn't just sit by. At least they were too stupid to do it right away; I guess they wanted to wait until the office was clear."

"How did you hear?"

Tommy just shrugged, glancing off.

She said, "Do you have a bug in the police department?"

He stared at her, his teardrop tattoo on the side of his eye drawing her attention.

"You don't have a *rat*, do you?" Artemis prompted again.

Tommy said, "How about we discuss your lawbreaking ways? Is it true you killed someone?"

"No!"

"So why did they think you did?"

"I don't know..." She trailed off, shifting where she stood on the porch, one foot creaking against the floorboards. She said, slowly, "That's not completely true. I do know. They have a video showing me killing him..."

Tommy whistled. "Shit—if I had known you were into that sort of action, I could've recommended a professional."

Artemis slapped a hand against the wooden rail that led up to the shed. "Don't be ridiculous. I didn't do it."

"You saying the footage was doctored?"

"It wasn't. One of my coworkers checked. It was the raw footage from the security company."

"So if they have you killing the guy on video, and the footage hasn't been doctored..." Tommy trailed off, raising his eyebrows at her.

"I know," she muttered. And then, like ripping off a band-aid, she said, "and that's not the only thing. They say they have my fingerprints on a gun registered in my name. There was blood on my sweater. His blood."

"The stiff's?"

"Yes!"

"So you did kill him. You don't have to lie. I've heard worse."

Artemis tightened her grip on the rail and felt splinters attempting to pierce her fingers. She relaxed her grip, deciding Tommy wasn't the only thing she didn't want under her skin. "I didn't kill anyone."

He studied her, crossing his arms and shifting his weight from one foot to the other. Then, he said, "So you're being set up?"

"Exactly!"

"How's that possible? Video footage, blood... help it make sense."

Artemis peered down the slope, staring vacantly in the direction of the river cutting through the red stone in the valley.

She could remember, years ago, coming here with their family. Once upon a time, when they had pretended to be normal.

Their father had been in a good mood that day.

Helen had been intent on catching the largest fish. Tommy had tried to get out of coming but had eventually been convinced by his sisters.

It had been a happy memory, for such a very long time. One of the things she hated most about her father was that he had taken away these memories. Every one of them was now tinted with darkness. Every one of them had a veneer of evil.

It had been cold, snow on the slopes, portions of the river iced over.

They had gone fishing, cutting holes in the ice, tossing a line through.

None of them had really known what they'd been doing.

Their father, like always, had spoken with such confidence, making things up as he went, that none of them had been the wiser until years later when they found out that there were no fish in this portion of the river. And that the best way to catch them was not through a hook draped through smashed ice.

But that was what her father had been good at; confidence, pretense—that was the reason so many people had believed him, had fallen for his tricks.

And so Artemis knew how easy it was to convince someone of something untrue.

The only problem was that usually such a ploy didn't have overwhelming physical evidence.

She shook her head in frustration.

"Do you believe me?"

Tommy stared, frowning instead of answering. Then he asked a question of his own. "Do *you* believe you?"

She felt a jolt of anxiety.

It was a fair question and a distinctly troubling one. Mulling over it... Did she believe? Or was she completely deluded?

Had she blacked out?

No. She could remember the meeting. Could remember the awkward encounter at the end. Could remember his threats. And then she'd left.

"Well," said Tommy, "if you are being set up and the murder is on camera, then it makes sense the best person to try to find is the guy you killed, right?"

Artemis shook her head. "He's dead. He was killed. Two gunshots to the chest. They found his body, apparently right after I left."

"I'm just not seeing it, sister. Follow the evidence, isn't that what they teach you?" He shook his head, moving away from his motorbike now and coming to a halt next to her outside the shed.

"If you thought I did it, why break me out? Also, a truck through the wall?"

He shrugged sheepishly. "Short notice. Best I could come up with."

"A month ago, you blew up a motorbike. This time you smash a wall with a truck. I'm beginning to think you might have a problem, Tommy." She had meant it to sound humorous, to lighten the mood.

Tommy even flashed a wry grin beneath the moon; his expression softened. She studied him, those familiar features, and yet, far older than she remembered. She felt a lance of regret. Guilt.

She knew Tommy blamed her for leaving. She knew he was still mad about it.

But she and her brother were so very different.

She said, with a sigh, "Thank you for helping me."

"That's what family is for," he said sarcastically.

Artemis said, "This might not be the best time. I know that, but what happened at the waterfall after I left?" The question had been burning in her mind. And despite her own concerns and temporary fears, she refused to let the issue go.

She paid a high price to get this clue from the Professor.

This time, instead of reacting with denial, Tommy said, slowly, "I've been thinking about that. And..." He sighed. He looked away, back towards the river, scratching at his long ponytail and then adjusting the collar of his leather jacket. "Do you know what these words mean?" he asked, pointing up at those face tattoos leading up from his neck past his cheeks.

Two words, in a language she didn't know. "Some sort of musical lyric?"

"That's your guess? Two words from a song?"

"No need to sound contemptuous, I'm not the one with the stupid face tattoo."

"Stupid?" He snorted and turned away.

"Sorry, look, sorry. I take it back. It's not stupid. It's very... unique."

"Now I think you just mean unique as another word for stupid."

"Tommy, don't be so sensitive."

He scowled at her. "Do you want to know the one way to make sure someone stops being sensitive?"

"What?"

"I don't know. But the opposite is to ask them not to be. This," he said, his voice cold, "is a combination of Syriac and Chinese. It's your name, Artemis."

As he said it, trailing a long finger over the faded tattoo, Artemis went quiet. She stared at her brother.

With an air of defiance, he moved his finger to his other cheek, jabbing hard until the skin indented. "And this is Helen."

Then he turned and began to yank down his pants.

"Wait," she squawked. "Yuck—what are you doing?"

He paused, half his ass revealed. "Want me to show you the tattoo I got of Dad's name?"

"No, absolutely not. You can just tell me about it."

Her brother pulled his pants up again, shrugging as if it was her loss. "Fine by me," he muttered. "I keep you two close. I never want to forget Helen, you—both of you were good people."

Artemis wasn't sure if she should feel touched or a little bit sad.

Both, she decided.

Her brother adjusted his belt and then crossed his arms.

"I didn't know those were our names. I'm sorry for calling it stupid."

Tommy just stared at her. "Well, it's in the past. But, you know what, sometimes, I would see you."

"Excuse me?"

He waved a hand as if it was no big deal. He rubbed at the bridge of his nose. "That's why I gotta ask, sis," he murmured. He looked at her with a sidelong glance. "How did you know about the waterfall?"

"So something *did* happen."

"You answer me, and I'll answer you."

"I didn't *know*. But someone told me... this... this killer, the Professor. He said I should ask you about Helen."

"Yeah... well... There's no way that creep should know." Tommy pulled at his face, his fingers tight against his skin. Then he shrugged once. "I used to see you too. In dreams... nightmares sometimes if Dad was in them." He shook his head, staring off towards the river and listening to the water.

Artemis didn't interject, listening quietly.

Tommy continued. "Well, shit, sis." He shook his head. "I would also sometimes see you when I was drunk... or sampling the supply if you catch my drift."

"Not sure I want to catch anything... What do you mean *see* us?"

He glanced at her. Another shoulder shrug. "I mean I'd see you wandering around. See you occasionally come in and out of focus. Only for a couple of years there. Haven't since."

"See us like... hallucinate?"

"I mean, shit. I don't know. You ever had mushrooms?"

"No."

"Well, that stuff is strong, sis. Can get you seeing all sorta weirdness. I saw dinosaurs too. Once saw the big donut on top of that gas station shop flying away on pegasus wings."

"I don't think I quite understand how—"

"I saw Helen."

"Oh... okay..."

"I thought it was just another apparition. You know... I was a little buzzed at the time. I was at the waterfall."

"The Shade Creek waterfall?"

"Yeah. Where the high schoolers gather. Road's too steep for most old folks. It's youngsters' territory up that way."

"How old were you at the time?"

"Sixteen. Something like. I was making some money."

Artemis bit her lip. She didn't want to inquire *how* her brother had made his living during his teen years. So instead, she said, "And what happened? You had a hallucination of Helen?"

"That... that was just it. I thought so. But..." He was now tapping his foot rapidly, clearly somewhat uncomfortable.

"But?" Artemis felt her own pulse quickening now. Responding to something in her brother's posture. To something like a haunted quality in his eyes.

Tommy said. "Big butt. Big ol' droopy ass, actually."

"What?"

"...But normally, the hallucinations didn't *give* me things. Which is why I'm creeped out this old killer you're talking about knew about it. I didn't tell a soul."

"About seeing Helen?"

"Nah... About what she gave me."

Artemis suddenly looked sharply up, meeting her brother's gaze. Her fingers were hurting, and it took her a second to notice her hand had shot out, gripping Tommy by the arm, tightly.

"What?" she demanded.

"Yeah," he shot back. "She gave me something. Don't know what it is. But I know she gave it." Artemis was still gripping her brother's leather-clad arm, but her eyes moved as his hand returned to his waist. Thank God, instead of pulling his pants down again to show an ass tattoo of their father's name, he reached into his waistband and pulled out a single wrinkled, white letter.

Judging by the state of the thing, with tears and crinkles and bent portions, it had been well read and poorly stored. But Tommy lifted the letter, allowing it to hover between them for a moment. She tried to snatch, but he pulled it back, and her hand missed.

"Hey!" she snapped. "Let me see? What is that!"

"Now, one second," Tommy said, still gripping the letter, his arm cocked to keep it out of reach from his sister. Artemis had flashbacks of more than one childhood experience. How many times had Tommy taken a favorite sweater or hat or the last piece of toaster pastry, keeping it out of arm's reach, if only to antagonize his twin sister.

But this...

This didn't feel the same. Tommy's eyes weren't full of mean mischief. Helen wasn't in the background, yelling for the two of them to simmer down before their Dad woke up. Artemis' stomach flipped as she studied her brother's expression.

Fear.

Lots of it.

The same fear she'd detected in his voice back at the party. But why?

She shifted uncomfortably, lowering her hand briefly. But then, as if unbidden, her hand shot up again, fingers uncurling to reach towards the envelope. "Please," she said. "Let me read it."

Tommy nibbled his lip. He hesitated. "Look... It's not... not something to be read. It's... just a weird picture. I need you to understand, sis... Helen didn't give me this. She couldn't have. I was just imagining her.

I once imagined you, about a year after you left, coming back and tossing water on my face while I was sleeping."

"Excuse me?"

"Yeah," he said. "You know... irritating things. Occasionally throwing water on me. Once, I had a dream of you kicking my toe. I woke up, and the damn thing was bruised. God's honest truth." He held up the hand with the letter towards the sky, as if making some divine proclamation.

But Artemis' eyes only narrowed. "How often would you imagine us? It's creepy, Tommy."

Now, he glared at her. "Here's me, baring my soul and you call me creepy?"

"No—I didn't mean it like that! Dammit, just let me see the letter."

"No. Hell no. Creepy! You call—shit, Art. I missed you guys. I had *no one*. Don't you get it, or are you just an idiot?" He was yelling now, his voice carrying down the mountain slopes, meeting the roar of the river. "I had *no one*. None. Nothing. You guys left, and I was alone. No, shut up, don't say anything. I'm not done."

"We've been over this!" Artemis retorted, despite his protest, remembering the last time they'd spoken back in Tommy's junkyard.

But he kept going. "You make a good impression wherever you go, Art. Everyone likes you. Everyone has. That damn room full of weirdos back at the ranch!"

"My friends!"

"Yes—exactly. Friends. Not all of us have those. Jamie was my only friend. I haven't seen the guy for years. Not really. When I was sixteen, Art, the cops in Pinelake were already making my life miserable. I had no friends. Had no family. Had *nothing*. So yeah—occasionally, my broken, little, drug-addled, piece of shit brain taunted me by reminding me I had once been happy. I saw you. Saw Helen. Saw Dad in my nightmares. It all sucked. I didn't ask for it. And it stopped after a couple of years. I got clean... well, mostly. Just some mild stuff nowadays."

"G-good for you," Artemis said, unsure what else to say. Her own mind was reeling, emotions whirring. She wanted to make it better for her brother. Wanted to tell him it was going to be okay. She also wanted to slap him and kick him in the shins then steal that letter he was waving about like a flag.

Neither of these options were realized, though, as her brother said, "And so, yeah, maybe it was weird. But I didn't ask for it. It wasn't all the time. It was sometimes. Maybe six or seven. Dunno. Saw you a few times, usually doing something to piss me off. Saw Helen a couple of times. But the one that creeped me out the most was—"

"This meeting at the waterfall. Where the hallucination gave you a letter. You know hallucinations can't do that, right? You... are you saying you actually saw Helen?"

"I... I mean... I don't know, Art. I really don't. Maybe someone else came up to me, and my mind thought of them as Helen."

"How buzzed were you?"

"What?"

"You said you were buzzed. How much?"

"Two thumbs up? Five stars? How would you like me to rank it, Art? You don't even drink, do you?"

"How would you know?"

"Internet. You got a buncha thirsty fanboys tracking your every move, sis."

She sighed, leaning back for a moment, head tilting. She couldn't bring herself to close her eyes. She didn't want to lose sight of that envelope in her brother's grip. If it really *was* a letter from Helen, then it was typical Tommy to not take care of the damn thing. If she looked close, it almost looked like he'd managed to spill some grease on it, smudging it with his thumb and ripping the corner.

She huffed in frustration, lowering her chin again.

"Are you done?" she said.

"Yeah."

"Sorry for calling it creepy," she said simply.

He scratched his chin. "Huh. Yeah, well..." he shrugged, glancing sheepishly off.

"Next time you want to rant at me, could you at least give me a chance to apologize *first,* that way you can conserve your breath. Feels like you used your monthly budget of words right there."

"Yeah, well…" he said again, this time not quite meeting her gaze.

Artemis wanted to add more. In a way, she wanted to shred into him the same way he had her. It wasn't her fault he didn't have friends. Wasn't her fault he didn't know how to play nice with others. For years, literally years, she and Helen had tried to coax Tommy into a less cynical, less rebellious attitude. He was the one who'd gone out of his way to flout every rule, to piss off every authority figure and to slap every hand ever offered to him.

It wasn't her fault he'd chosen to be a drug dealer by the age of sixteen. That he'd figured out how to get on the bad side of law enforcement long before the news about the Ghost-killer broke. It wasn't her damn fault he'd never learned to express his emotions, had chosen to never *tell* her how much he needed her around.

She'd left Pinelake because he'd cozied up with criminals. Because he'd made his crooked damn bed, and she wasn't about to stick around to watch him die too.

And even as she thought all of this, wanting to give voice to it, she couldn't…

For the simple fact that she still felt guilty. As much as she wanted to give as good as she'd gotten, she'd always thought of Tommy as the baby of the family.

They were twins. Helen had been the oldest...

But Tommy... he was... she was the one who'd protected him. Helen and her. The two of them had always tried to back their brother up. Had even hidden him from police, on more than one occasion, or stepped in, defending him before some school jock could pummel him for trying to sleep with one of their girlfriends.

Tommy just didn't make decisions the same way others did. He'd always been a bit of a wise-ass...

Artemis huffed in frustration. She couldn't help but notice those two stupid face tattoos again. But now... looking at them, they didn't irritate her. The names of his sisters. Helen and Artemis... if he was telling the truth, that was. But she believed him. Knowing her brother, it made sense.

The only two people he'd ever... loved in his fashion.

And in his mind, they'd abandoned him.

And in a way...

Artemis sighed. They had.

She stared at the tattoos, her eyes lingering on the one he'd said stood for Artemis. She swallowed, biting back her need to defend herself. Her desire to exchange insults.

She tried to think of some little advice Helen might have given in that moment. But it didn't come. Artemis' mind was still spinning.

If that letter *really had* been from Helen... She stared at it, watching where it fluttered in the mountain breeze.

"Can I see it?" she said at last, tilting her head inquisitively.

Tommy studied her. He said, "I don't know if it was from her. There were a bunch of teenagers handing me stuff that day. Sometimes I-Owe-You notes in favor for a dimebag or two."

"I get it. You might have imagined it. But you didn't imagine *that*. So can I see it?"

Tommy scratched at his chin, his fingers trailing beneath his tattoos. Then he grunted, extending the letter towards her. This time, when she reached to accept it, he didn't jerk his hand back.

Trembling, her fingers shaking the letter, she opened it. She pulled out a folded piece of cream paper. Instantly, she recognized the stationery. It had come from a set that Artemis and Helen had saved up for and bought together. Some of their savings had come from loose change Tommy had taken from the coat pockets of audience members at their father's mentalism shows. Neither sister had turned down the help.

Now, still shaking badly, Artemis unfolded the paper and stared at the contents of the single page. The sheet, years ago, would have vaguely exuded the fragrance of heather. But the perfume had long since faded, and yet, in her mind, Artemis could still conjure the memory. The image of the two girls sitting excitedly on their bed, both of them eagerly unhooking the plastic clasps of the stationery box, opening it and delightedly handing items from the box back and forth.

She could still remember Helen pausing, holding a beige envelope to her nose and whispering, *"Oh, wow… it's like summer."*

As Artemis stood there, holding the familiar paper between shaking fingers, she felt a lump forming in her throat. Tommy was watching her closely, the moon joined in, the trees seemed to shiver a bit more quietly, as if sensing the solemnity of the moment.

Artemis studied the note itself, eyes fixated. It wasn't a written note. At least, *not* exactly.

Chapter Seven

D4. D6. NF3. NC6....

And on and on it went. She frowned, shaking her head.

"See," Tommy muttered. "It's not even a letter... just... pointless numbers."

"It's chess annotation," Artemis said quickly.

"Right, I know that," Tommy said crossly.

"You did?" she looked up.

He hesitated, then shrugged. "I mean... I could've guessed that."

She sighed in frustration. Tommy had *never* been interested in chess the same way the two girls had. Every time Helen had tried to include him in their little lessons, he'd refused and left the house to do his own thing. Usually that thing involved breaking a municipal code or three.

"This *is* from Helen!" Artemis said firmly. "The paper, the annotati on... You *saw* her!"

"I imagined her," he shot back. "Same as I imagined you. Same as I imagined Dad, even while he was behind bars."

Artemis shook her head. "I'm not saying you didn't imagine some of them but not this one. It isn't possible. It's the same stationery. She wrote annotation—Tommy. It's a code! She's speaking to us."

Artemis' voice rose in excitement, but Tommy just watched her, his expression grim.

"I mean..." he trailed off. "Maybe." He sounded doubtful.

And Artemis allowed a bit of his uncertainty to rain on her parade. She frowned, glancing at the letter again. She'd already spent some time attempting to figure out postcards. Attempting to crack her father's code. It had turned out, the cards themselves had no code. It was the drugs laced into the cards—hallucinogens used by her father to bribe prisoners and guards. To keep his marionettes twitching beneath his fingers.

She'd discovered what he'd been up to the previous month and promptly gone to the warden. The warden had confiscated any other cards and interviewed any prisoner found with them on their persons, under the threat of losing privileges or having further charges brought against them.

A familiar story had arisen. A corrupt prison guard nicknamed *Easy* had been the main associate with the Ghost-killer's drug-running business. Last she'd checked, the warden still hadn't managed to discover *Easy's* identity.

Once they did, Artemis felt confident, her father's machinations would be discovered. His plans would be stopped—whatever those were. The Ghost-killer was always cooking up something.

Now, though, studying this new envelope, she felt certain... Helen hadn't laced the paper. Helen wasn't trying to deceive.

Helen wanted to communicate.

And judging by the annotation... Helen wanted to communicate with Artemis. Who else would she be speaking to with snapshots of chess openings?

Indeed, there were *eight separate* chess openings listed on the paper. Artemis frowned as she studied each of the openings, trying to make sense.

"These... these are games we played," Artemis murmured, frowning.

"What?"

"Helen and I," Artemis shot back. "These are games *we* played!" her voice was growing agitated as she spoke. She stared, trying to make sense of it, trying to remember each opening and the corresponding game she had played with Helen.

"Each of them is improvised. None of them are standard lines. This was before I learned any of that..."

"And?" Tommy said.

"And! Helen is communicating; she wanted me to have this!" Artemis' eyes flashed, and she stared at Tommy. She lowered the paper for a moment. "Why didn't you give this to me?"

He glared back. "Why did you leave Pinelake if you wanted me to give it to you?"

"I didn't know you had it!"

"Yeah, well, tough eggs."

"What?" Artemis' temper flared again.

"I'm giving it to you now," Tommy shot back. "I didn't know it was from Helen."

"You said you saw her!" Artemis yelled.

"I said," he replied, bluntly, "I imagined her. Hallucinated. That's all. The creepy part is that this old serial killer of yours knew about it. Wanna wonder *why*? Because maybe he's the one playing with you, Art. Maybe he's the one who gave that to me. I don't know. I don't remember."

"Because you were high! Because you were hallucinating while *high*!"

"Because I was sixteen. Not all of us try to remember every damn thing in life, Art. Some of us, believe it or not, spend most our time *trying* to forget. Hell, I forgot I even had that until you brought up the waterfall back at your little party."

Artemis wanted to slap her brother. She wanted to scream at the moon in frustration. But she also knew she needed to think rationally. There was no sense losing her temper. No sense getting furious over something outside her control.

Tommy should have given this letter to her. But...

"So when did you get this? *When*?"

"Umm... I think a year after you bailed."

"After I left Pinelake?"

"Yes!"

"So that... that would have been nearly four years after Helen disappeared."

"Three, I think. About. Yeah."

Artemis clicked her tongue. "And you didn't think this was worth mentioning?"

"Hey—I *did* mention it."

"To who?"

"Sheriff Dawkins. The cops. Who else? I told them my sister was around—a missing minor. They said to bug off."

"You did?"

"Yeah," Tommy snapped. "But like I'm saying, I didn't press the issue, because I didn't know if it was her or not. I still don't."

"I'm telling you it is! Who else would have this stationery? Who else would know those matches I played with her?"

Tommy shrugged. Then, his voice monotone, like a dull hammer pounding old wood, he said simply, "Someone who kidnapped her, tortured her and wanted to screw with us."

Artemis went quiet. Tommy did too. They both stared at each other.

Artemis swallowed, her hand having fluttered like the wing of a dying bird down to her waist. She gripped the edge of the stationery and said, slowly, "That was a cruel thing to say."

"But maybe true. Art, this place is sick. The people around here... there's killers. Dad was one. But think about Jamie's old man. Think about this guy who *knew* about what happened at the waterfall."

Artemis trailed off, feeling a lancing pain in her chest. Was Tommy right? Was the Professor using some manufactured memory to play with her? Was Tommy misremembering after all these years?

But... but how? It would have taken *so* many coincidences.

The Professor just so happened to know about Tommy's hallucination of his sister? That was the linchpin, wasn't it.

"Tommy," she said quietly.

"Huh?"

"Did you... I'm serious. Try to remember. Did you tell *anyone* about seeing Helen, *before* you did?"

"I..." he paused. Then shrugged. "Might have come up a couple of times. Drinking. But just with strangers."

And it was like a balloon deflating. Artemis closed her eyes, loosing pent up air. Drinking with strangers. If someone interested in taking advantage had heard about Tommy's meeting with Helen...

The Professor hadn't said anything about a note, though.

Then again, what if he'd been the one to plant it? Hell... what if he'd hired someone who *looked* like Helen just to screw with Tommy. Clearly the old, depraved killer had an interest in the Blythe family.

Hell... had an interest in her old man. Artemis didn't even know what to make of the claims of connection between the Professor and her family... her father. Herself.

Was he somehow playing with them? Was her father involved?

Maybe this had been part of her father's way of attempting to get at Artemis. At Tommy. She wouldn't have put it past the Ghost-killer to pull something like this just to screw with them...

There were forms of manipulation, of hypnosis that could conjure dream-like trances. Could bring to mind images of long lost kin. F riends... sisters...

Artemis didn't know what to think, which was one of the cruelties of growing up as a Blythe. Her old man had twisted things so badly, she didn't even know which way was up and which was down.

Tommy had seen Helen, though. It might have been imaginary...but the letter proved it wasn't, didn't it? *Something* had happened.

"I... I think she might still be alive," Artemis said firmly. She didn't voice the other options. Didn't give credence to Tommy's own claim. Another horrible thought had occurred to her, that maybe Helen really had been alive, three years after her kidnapping. Maybe she'd managed to break free of her captors in time to give this letter to Tommy, hoping—somehow—Artemis might read it. Might save her.

And maybe, since Artemis had left Pinelake, she'd never received the letter. And so Helen's plea had been left unanswered.

Fifteen years, nearly, had passed since the supposed incident at the waterfall.

Even if Helen had been alive then, there was no saying she was still alive.

Artemis' stomach twisted.

She raised Tommy's letter once more, committing it entirely to memory. She scanned the envelope, the rest of the paper, committing any imperfection to recollection as well, studying not just the picture, but the frame, and the chips of paint *around* the frame. Anything that might be used to communicate.

As she did this, under the scrutiny of her twin brother, a weight of exhaustion settled heavily on her. Artemis inhaled shakily, holding the breath before releasing it again.

This was all just too much.

She'd wanted to find a clue to Helen's whereabouts. And now... now it felt like she really had one. She felt a jolt of frustration that she'd allowed the Professor, the prolific killer, to escape. She'd been attempting to aid Forester and Wade at the time, and it had seemed like the right choice.

But now, her heart pining for her sister, Artemis couldn't help but regret allowing John Kordan to escape. He would have had the answers. How did he know about Tommy's interaction with Helen? Was it really Helen? What was the letter?

If anyone knew, it was him.

But this wasn't the only troubling puzzle.

A far more immediate and pressing threat loomed on the horizon.

Artemis Blythe... murderer.

That was the story now circling the Pinelake police department. If the Dawkins family didn't *already* have a reason to hate her, then they certainly did now.

Ross Dawkins had intended her harm, in the heart of his own sheriff's department.

This alone was enough to send shivers up her spine. Artemis gnawed on her lower lip, shifting her stance and shooting a quick look towards Tommy. Exhaustion... too much exhaustion. Too much weight.

"I... Tommy... I need your help," she said quietly. The moment she did, she winced.

Her brother studied her, his face expressionless. His usual mask had returned, his eyes half hooded. And when he replied, the emotion had vanished from his voice as well; he spoke again with laconic sentences. "Mhmm. What?"

"Can I keep this?" she said to start with.

He glanced at her, at the letter. For a moment, he looked ready to refuse. He scratched at his face tattoo again, though, then muttered. "Fine. A grand."

"What?"

"I'll give it to you for a grand."

"You're joking."

He didn't blink, didn't smile, just watched her. "I'll take it back if not."

"Fine!" she said quickly. "I'll pay you. I still have some from winning the Seattle Open."

"Dunno what that means. But pay me first, then I'll give it back."

"I—I can't do it *now.*"

He shrugged, extending his fingers now, snapping them. She stared incredulously at her brother. This had always been the problem with Tommy. One moment vulnerable and angry, the next cold and indifferent. But still, she *did* need his help. Her normal channels of aid were now cut off to her.

The FBI, for one, would arrest her on sight.

And the Pinelake sheriff's department?

She shivered at the mere thought.

She said, "I... I don't have my phone. Or wallet. Or any of it. It was all confiscated."

"Yeah well," Tommy shrugged. His hand snatched out, his fingerless gloves a black blur as he grabbed the letter back. It nearly ripped, but Artemis instantly released it to avoid damaging the precious note.

She watched, forlorn as Tommy slipped it back in his waistband. "You can have it for a grand," he said firmly. "Payment upfront."

"You're... a real ass, you know that?"

"I just risked my neck breaking you out of prison. Trucks aren't cheap."

"A grand says you *stole* that truck."

"Yeah, well... The risk could have been costly." Tommy shook his head now, tucking his shirt in again, hiding the note except for the faintest outline.

As much as she wanted to slap him, to lash out, Artemis knew that antagonizing her brother was a good way to get him to do something stupid. Like burning the thing while she watched. There was residue of fifteen-year-old Tommy still there. But this was a man, now. A man who'd lived half his life thumbing his nose at anyone who might even whisper, "Should" or "Ought" or "Must."

There was a calcifying effect that came with a life of middle-fingers to the *man.*

She shook her head, briefly double-checking that she had managed to properly memorize the thing. She'd done the best she could.

She shook her head, shooting a final forlorn look at the faint outline of a rectangle against her brother's shirt. But then, she said, "I need your help with something else."

"What?"

"Well…" she exhaled slowly as she said it, and it felt as if she were relieving both pent-up stress and deep frustration. But only one problem could be handled at a time. As much as she wanted to look into that envelope, she needed access to her phone. Needed the money Tommy demanded, but also needed the space to move about, to visit places without fearing that, at any moment, she might be arrested and attacked in a Dawkins prison cell.

No. She needed to clear her name. And *then* she could figure out this business with Helen. Part of her mind was already piecing together the eight separate openings she'd had. Trying to remember the games they'd played. Trying to remember what had been said, what had been done... Why Helen might have chosen *those* openings.

If it really was Helen.

She hissed in frustration, again feeling her stomach twist in knots.

One enemy at a time.

"I didn't kill him," she said firmly.

"You sure?"

"I don't hallucinate."

"So why does it look like you killed him?"

"The answer," she said, "with the most likely explanation is where we need to focus."

"The most *likely* explanation," her brother said, trailing off.

"I didn't."

"So second most likely?"

"Look at it how you want," she snapped. "But obviously I'm being set up."

The moment she said it, laying it bare, displaying it like a small, crumpled flower unfurling on her palm, she felt a weight release from her shoulders.

A set-up.

It had to be.

What other option was there?

Someone was setting her up. Someone wanted her arrested for the murder of Azin... but who?

Tommy, deciding to temporarily play nice with others, muttered, "I mean... I can think of a few people who hate your guts. But... if you think it's a set-up... You gotta ask yourself one thing... Who hated Azin enough to get him killed? And who hates you enough to frame you for it?"

But Artemis shook her head. "Maybe Azin had nothing to do with it. Maybe he was just a useful pawn."

"Pawn. I know that one."

"Yes, the least valuable piece in chess... until the end game. Then it becomes the most valuable."

"Sure. So, who wanted Azin dead? And who wanted you in prison. Those are the two potential motives. And the second one, you think, narcissistically I might add, is the more likely?"

She rankled at this accusation but just nodded.

He snorted, turning back towards his motorcycle. "Well damn, sis. That's easy. Everyone knows who wanted you in prison. They've wanted that for nearly two decades."

"Who?"

He paused, adjusting his driving gloves over his fingerless ones. He shot her a look, raising an eyebrow under his flyaway hair. "Who just tried to murder you in a cell?"

"Ross Dawkins?" Artemis snorted. "Ross is too stupid to tie his own shoes without a how-to guide."

"Doesn't gotta just be Ross. Merl is the brains of that operation."

"His scrawny brother?"

"Could be."

Artemis shot back. "Or, more likely, Sheriff Dawkins. It's his wife that Dad killed."

Tommy shrugged. "Or Sergeant Larry. His mom."

Artemis paused. "Or maybe all of them combined," she said. "Do you really think they'd go to this much trouble to get me arrested? They'd kill someone like Azin?"

"I mean... maybe. What about Azin himself?"

"I thought of that. But he's dead. Why would he set me up just to get himself killed?" Artemis hesitated, then answered her own question. "Unless he was in on it from the start," she murmured. "And he was double-crossed?"

"So what about that video?" Tommy said.

Artemis huffed a sigh. "I was... thinking about that. I remember *most* of that horrible experience. But not the last part. The last part was made-up. Staged."

"Some look-alike hired to play you?"

Artemis said. "But the footage was *live*. The whole thing was live. The security company provided the raw footage."

Tommy said. "I mean... there's a couple of ways to approach that."

Artemis nodded quickly. "I know. But... do we rule the security company out? Maybe someone there is in on it. Bribed?"

"Could be. What company?"

"I... I don't know." She bit her lip.

"Who *does*?"

"Well..." Artemis trailed off. She'd always hated the expression of killing two birds with one stone. What had the poor birds ever done to anyone? And what schmuck was using stones to peg 'em? But in this case... She wouldn't have minded a couple of rocks chucked at *these* particular birds. "One of the Dawkins," she said simply. "They hate me. Hate our family. Ross and Merl were going to hurt me. If anyone's behind it, it's them."

"Could be Dad," Tommy said.

Artemis scowled now. A few good theories already, which was only expanding the terrain. Was the Ghost-killer behind this, using his connections from inside the prison, a guard named *Easy*, to manipulate the world outside those gray fenced-in walls, to mess with his daughter? Maybe this was payback for cutting off his postcard supply. Maybe he wanted her in prison.

Or what about the Dawkins family? They clearly weren't above twisting the law, outright shattering it, to get what they wanted, to settle a blood feud.

And on top of it, what about Azin? Was he in on it? Especially remembering his accusations at the end of the meeting. Telling her he was going to report her. That he refused to play in a tournament with someone like her... Had he been in on it then double-crossed?

A few things were clear.

She needed to confirm Azin was actually dead. Needed to find out if he'd been in contact with her father or anyone associated with the prison. And she needed to find out *what* security company had handled the footage.

Tampered footage. That was the only explanation.

The blood on her sweater, the gun registered in her name, the fingerprints on the gun... All of that could be handled at a later date.

For now...

One step at a time.

"I need... need to borrow your phone," she said.

"Hell no."

"Tommy!"

"No! You're calling a fed."

"I... well..."

"Yeah, see. I knew it. I'm not letting you call a fed. I'll give you a ride. I've already done my part, sis. You do your thinking thing. I break stuff. Simple."

She snorted. "You're not a fool, and the only one you're kidding is yourself. Fine. I'll find a phone. I need you to drop me off somewhere, though."

"Then what?"

"I'm going to get some information. Confirm some things. Then... I think you're right. I need to look into the Dawkins."

Tommy made an expression like sucking lemons. "You think that's smart?"

"No. But I have to."

"If they see you sneaking around, they'll ventilate you, Art."

"I know. So they'd best not see me. Now about that ride..."

"Where to?"

She considered this for a moment, wincing as she did. She knew she didn't want to involve him. Knew it was a mistake to bring him in... But it wasn't like she had many friends left in the area. And Tommy's good graces were neither good nor very gracious. He'd done what he'd wanted to—he'd helped her, but he wouldn't go further.

No... she needed someone a bit less mule-headed. And she could only think of one person who wasn't a fed that Tommy might be willing to contact.

"I need you to make a call."

"I already said—"

"Not to a fed. To a friend. And we need to be cryptic. No doubt they're watching his phone."

Tommy shook his head, gesturing for her to approach the motor-bike. "I mean, you tell me who and what, and I'll tell you if."

"Hmm?"

"What message?"

Artemis paused, considering this, then doubling her pace as she approached the bike. It was still dark, night still stretched across the sky. There was time... Not much. But time.

All she needed was a little bit of information.

Chapter Eight

She watched as Tommy disappeared along the road curving past the pond. The sputtering of his motorbike accompanied the billowing of his jacket sleeves. She stood with her fingers tapping on the worn rail, her eyes moving across a low mist creeping over the pond and stretching across the tarmac of the cracked parking lot.

She inhaled shakily, breathing the fresh air and desperately hoping it wouldn't be her last.

It was evident by the speed in which Tommy fled that he wasn't nearly so confident in the trust she'd placed. But Artemis wasn't worried about Jamie Kramer betraying her.

She was more worried that she hadn't been cryptic enough in her text, or that Jamie might not be able to give the cops the slip.

Still... a risk had to be taken.

She was swimming up a creek without a paddle, and a boat filled with holes. She needed a break.

The message had been a simple one. *The kiss. There. Careful. Very careful. Also remember how we spoke for a couple of weeks, I need that.*

The translation clear enough, she felt. Meet where we kissed last. And I need a phone.

Jamie was smart, but the message was cryptic. It had to be. The FBI was undoubtedly watching. Agent Butcher had struck Artemis as a fair woman but a harsh one.

In some ways, the pinch-faced FBI operative had reminded Artemis of Agent Grant.

And so now it was with some unease that Artemis shifted uncomfortably in the gazebo by the pond, watching the empty parking lot, the swirl of the mist, and listening to the sputter of her brother's motorbike as it escaped the road, back into the forest.

And then silence came.

Whispers followed.

But she refused to give in. One enemy at a time. The cold nipped at her skin. She watched the road, prepared to make a run for it at any moment if she spotted anything untoward. Another reason she'd chosen the pond-side gazebo was because there was only one road in, and it was visible for nearly a mile. The forest was close enough, and she still remembered most of the trails through these mountains.

The Wishing Well property and its ominous mountain weren't far from here either.

She shivered, remembering the bodies they'd found beneath those trees and in that empty mineshaft.

"Focus," she murmured to herself.

Her mind kept rebelling against the cajoling. It wanted to think about Helen. About the Professor.

But she had to take things one step at a time. Like any good match, things could change at a moment's notice. Preparing sixteen moves in advance, ideating on the fifteenth or fourteenth, could leave her entirely unprepared for move three or eight.

One step at a time.

Holding plans loosely.

She was aided in this endeavor by a flash of lights. She froze. The lights blinked off and on, glaring towards her as it approached.

She hesitated, swallowing. She didn't recognize the car...

Then again, she *had* told Jamie to be careful. Maybe he'd borrowed someone's vehicle. She watched as the car approached, tense, preparing to bolt at any second. The vehicle came to a halt not far from her, the bright lights glaring at the gazebo for a few seconds longer than was strictly necessary.

Artemis raised her hand, wincing and blocking out the light.

She hesitated, flinching. And then a figure pushed out of the front of the vehicle, shielding his own eyes. He muttered to himself, reached back in and flicked off the lights, retrieved his keys and slammed the door.

The mist swirled about him, making a ghost of his figure for a moment. But then, Artemis' heart settled, and she breathed a sigh of relief as Jamie Kramer hurried towards her, slipping the keys into his pocket and, in his other hand, pulling a phone.

He was frowning as he drew nearer. Once he met her gaze, though, his expression softened. His sea gray eyes flicked back over his shoulder, towards the parking lot, as if determining whether they were still alone.

He moved hastily, a quick spring to his step.

Artemis watched as he drew near, her lips pressed tight. Her heart bounced in her chest. She felt equal parts relieved and, in an odd way, warm. Jamie Kramer had come for her. He'd understood the message. And, judging by that small flip phone in his hand, he'd discerned the rest of it too.

He took a couple of skipping steps over cracked stones, hastening towards her. As he drew near, though, he went still, frowning.

Artemis frowned too, peering past him.

The two of them both went suddenly still. Another car had appeared on the road. She hadn't spotted it until too late, as it had been evidently moving up the road with the headlights off, despite the late hour and treacherous visibility.

Jamie gripped the phone tightly in one hand, eyes widening. For one moment, she thought he might try and chuck the thing into the pond. But then, he turned, gesturing urgently at her. He didn't speak, didn't seem to want to make any sound at all. He just gestured, already fumbling to retrieve his keys.

But it was too late. The dark car had emerged at the end of the parking lot now, was coming hastily towards them. They had to run. To the woods. But Jamie was ten paces up the path. Too far for her to reach. She waved at him, hissing sharply beneath her breath.

But he was still distractedly waving at her.

Calamity.

He wasn't coming towards her. Artemis was outside the gazebo now, tensed briefly. She needed to turn, to run. No time to grab Jamie.

But of course she couldn't leave him. He'd risked everything for her. And so, with a sinking sensation in her stomach, she hastened forward, snatching at Jamie's arm. The car had now parked. The door flung open.

She yanked at Jamie, who was equally trying to pull her towards his vehicle—the headlights flashing suggesting he'd used an automatic lock opener.

"Come on," she whispered in his ear. "We have to run!"

Jamie looked at her, startled, but nodded quickly, and began to turn.

But a voice called after them, punctuated by the slamming door of the vehicle. "You two look real cozy," the voice called.

Artemis heart skipped a beat. She winced, recognizing that playful drawl. The tone completely out of place in the misty night. Then again, Agent Forester had never exactly been a man of decorum.

For one wild moment, she thought to sprint away anyway. But Forester was fast. And Jamie was still confused, panicked. He'd come to help her. Brought the phone. But in the end, he wasn't the one training to work with the FBI.

He was a kindhearted man. Not a killer.

A killer, on the other hand, was stalking straight towards them now, whistling *Twinkle, Twinkle Little Star* beneath his breath as he approached, his hands jammed in his jean pockets. He was still wearing the obnoxious Hawaiian shirt he'd been wearing back at the party.

"So," Forester said as he drew near. Artemis tensed, deciding last minute to simply face the FBI agent. "Guess that tip was useful."

Chapter Nine

Artemis paused, she swallowed. She didn't want to speak. A silly thought—he clearly had already recognized them. She was an escaped murder suspect—he was an FBI agent. And so, she dropped the silent act, and said, "Hey, Forester. Nice night for a stroll."

Jamie was tensed at her side. Muttering beneath his breath, "Shit, shit, shit."

She tried to squeeze his arm, to let him know it was going to be okay, but this only seemed to panic him further, and he took the squeeze as a cry for help, causing him to give her a quick once-over, making sure she was okay.

"I'm fine," she muttered. "Forester's... not... dangerous. Well, no, he is." She cut herself off, exhaling. "Why are you here, Cam?"

"Oh, dunno. Like the pond at night. Dreamy moonscape forest. The usual. How 'bout yourself?" He was still speaking chipper, but his eyes were shrewd, narrowed and cold, like a snake about to strike.

She swallowed delicately, still standing very close to Jamie. Forester seemed to notice this too. He watched them both, his eyes studying where they pressed against one another. He paused momentarily, gave a little exhale through his nostrils and glanced off, spitting on the ground.

"It's not what it looks like," Artemis said quickly.

"A little romantic tryst at night?"

"Umm... what? No—not... not with Jamie. I mean the..." she paused, trailing off. It struck her as odd that Forester had interpreted her words to be a defense for her actions with Jamie. This opened a whole kettle of fish she absolutely did not want to examine. So she slipped seamlessly past, ignoring the clear inference. "Ross Dawkins nearly killed me in my prison cell. My brother... I mean... someone..."

"Huh. I knew it was Tommy," said Forester. "Don't worry, you didn't rat him. He's the one who mentioned I ought to keep an eye on Mr. Kramer here."

"He what?" Artemis demanded.

Forester nodded. He lifted his phone, cleared his throat as if reciting a line from a play and read, "My sis gonna meet Jamie. Follow him. Bring a phone." He glanced back at Artemis, raising an eyebrow.

"Tommy sent you that?" she said, scandalized.

"Yup."

"Bastard," she snapped.

"Hey, don't shoot the messenger," he said.

"I meant Tommy." She glared off into the night along the road Tommy had disappeared up. He'd texted an FBI agent without telling her. The nerve of that punk.

"My guess," Forester said, "is he knew you'd need some muscle, yeah? He seemed to peg me for someone who might skirt a rule or two." Forester sounded aggrieved.

"Good judge of character, then," Artemis muttered. "I never thought I'd say that of Tommy."

"What... what's going on here," Jamie said, glancing between the two of them. "You are FBI, right?" he demanded, frowning at Forester.

"That's right. But, you know... I don't mind watching until the credits roll. See what happens."

"What?" Jamie demanded, his voice going somewhat higher. But he steadied himself now and took a protective step between Artemis and Forester, standing in the curling mist, under the bright moon, and clenching his fists at his sides. "I won't let you turn her in!" he snapped. "Ov-over my dead body!" His voice shook but steadied at the end.

Artemis was touched. Forester was snickering, which somewhat ru-ined the gesture.

"What?" Jamie snapped. Clearly he didn't like being laughed at. And creeping around with fugitives under the cover of night was *not* his area of expertise. He stepped back, wrapping an arm around Artemis' waist in a defensive stance. At least... *mostly* defensive. But also... if Artemis didn't know better, she might have thought Jamie was staking a claim.

Forester stopped chuckling, though. And now the two men were once more glaring at each other. Artemis wasn't entirely sure what sort of testosterone-telekinesis was occurring, so she cut to the point. "Are you going to take me in, Cam?"

"Not sure yet," he said. "Why did you need a phone?"

"To make a call," she shot back. "To you."

"Me?"

"Him?" Jamie demanded.

Artemis winced. "Yes, you. I need help, Forester. To clear my name. I didn't do this."

"You keep saying that," Forester replied. "But..." he raised a single, pale finger. "Got you on video doing it. Got your fingerprints on your murder weapon. Got video of you chucking the murder weapon into a bush where Agent Butcher found it. Got the victim's blood on your sweater." He kept four fingers waving beneath his chin now, as if waiting for some sort of response.

Artemis puffed air. A little curl of mist swirled past her lips.

Jamie was still holding on to her, his arm warm against the small of her back. But by the time Forester had listed his third finger, Jamie shot her a quick look. His grip loosened somewhat. He stared at her, and Artemis could *feel* his questions burning.

She couldn't blame him. But the doubt in his eyes hurt.

Still, Jamie's own father had killed his mother. At the time, Kramer had taken his father's side in some of the parental disputes. Artemis wasn't sure he'd been able to forgive himself for this. Mr. Kramer had been used by the Ghost-killer to get at her. Distrusting loved ones was par for the course in Pinelake.

Jamie kept his arm where it was but beneath his breath, he murmured, "They have a video?"

"Has to be fake," Artemis whispered.

"Oh... yeah... Of course," Jamie said, sounding relieved.

"Nah," Forester called out. "Can't be fake. They got the raw—"

"Security footage from the company," Artemis shot back. "I *know*. Which is why I needed to call you, Cam. I need to know that company's name."

"Huh," Forester said. "Great minds think alike."

"What?"

"See," Cameron replied. "That's what I thought. Someone at the company *must* have messed with it, right? Except the company in question stores the footage in three encrypted cloud servers, completely inaccessible to employees. On top of it, I checked already. The employees are squeaky clean. No mystery deposits. No correspondence with anyone in the area. The nearest employee lives in Bangladesh." Forester rattled all of this off in something of a bored tone.

Artemis, though, felt as if she'd been struck. "So you're saying..." she murmured. "Even if someone had been at the security company, they couldn't have altered the video?"

"I'm saying," Forester replied, "That not only could anyone have altered the video. But also, no one at the company had any motive to. I'd stake my sexy smile on it."

"Who is this guy?" Jamie muttered in disgust.

Artemis tried to return the half hug, but she was also trying to put her thoughts in order. Her stomach was twisting, and she felt deflated.

If no one had doctored the video footage, then it narrowed down her options substantially. There were no gaps in the video. The story it told was very different than the one Artemis remembered.

Which meant...

"Either," she said slowly, "I'm completely deluded. I am out of my mind, and I forgot what happened..."

"Or?" Jamie said urgently.

"Or," she replied, "that video was faked... and," she said quickly, "It must have been faked *after* I left Azin's house."

"How do you mean?" Forester asked.

"I mean," Artemis replied. "Whatever happened on that video is fake. I never shot him. I never said those things at the end. It's telling in the video that we can only see *me* from the side. Nothing is in focus. Not really."

"When you step outside," Forester pointed out.

Artemis hesitated but only for a moment. Sometimes, the most obvious answer was the right one. She said, "Is the outside camera the *same* as the inside security system?"

Forester scratched his chin. He was slow about it, but he reached into his pocket, pulled out his phone and began glancing through somewhat quickly. Artemis waited impatiently. Forester paused every few moments, and finally, he frowned so deeply she thought he might lose an eyebrow to his eye.

"What?" she said.

"Not the same," he muttered. He looked up. "The outside camera is just a little doorcam that feeds to Mr. Kartov's own phone."

"Bingo," Artemis said, excited now. "Do you have timestamps?"

"Hmm?"

"I noticed on the videos I was shown there were no timestamps."

Forester glanced at his phone again, muttering. He then said, "File is still in Butcher's purview. I don't have permissions yet. Just screenshots of the information."

Jamie cleared his throat, cutting Forester off and saying, "Why is that important, Artemis? Different companies for the cameras? Timestamps?"

"Yeah," she said quickly, nodding and frowning. "It's the only thing that makes sense. I *do* show up on the outside footage. And I *do* throw something in the garden. It wasn't a gun, though. It was a tube of photos."

"Right. The photos you mentioned Azin gave you."

"Exactly. He wanted me to quit the tournament. He wanted me to know he'd found out about my Dad. He seemed disgusted by my parentage."

Jamie was scowling, shaking his head now.

Forester had a more cautious look, his eyes shining like a wolf's in the night. "So Azin gave you something and you flung it into the garden?"

"Yes," Artemis said firmly. "Which means someone saw that, placed the gun there instead, removed the pictures... and," she said quickly, "that must have been how they got my fingerprints!" She nodded in excitement.

But Forester bust her bubble. "Don't think so. This the roll of photos?" He pulled a plastic bag out of his back pocket and held it up for her to see.

She stared at the small, cardboard tube. Then she nodded. "Looks like it."

"I see," Forester trailed off, sighing. "Alright. I won't turn you in."

Artemis felt a surge of relief. Jamie, though, still looked irritated.

Forester wiggled the tube so they could see, causing some of the mist to swirl as if being disturbed by a conductor's wand. Forester clicked his tongue, shaking his head and frowning at the two of them. "You know," he murmured slowly, "I went back to Azin's place. Checked out the crime scene, looked where you said to. Found this thing wedged between two branches."

Artemis just watched him.

Forester crossed his arms, his palm flashing and revealing the pale stain of his scar. He reached up, rubbing absentmindedly at an ear that had been ruined by boxing. "Took me nearly half an hour to find that," he said. "In the dark. Nearly gave up myself—but then I saw it, wedged there, in the branches, completely obscured."

Artemis stared at him. "You looked for that for half an hour?"

"Yup. Good thing, too. My guess..." he trailed off, "either you killed Azin and are playing all of us—"

"I didn't!"

"She didn't!" Jamie yelled. Though his arm was still rigid. His words were confident, his body language not so much. She hated admitting how much it hurt to realize this. It wasn't his fault, of course; she knew he couldn't help himself, but still...

Forester said, "Well, then... the second option is that some nefarious actors, for whatever reason, have gone to great lengths to checkmate your pawn-rookie."

"That sentence makes no sense."

He continued as if he hadn't heard, pacing back and forth now, nodding as he did. "But I am the real king! The most powerful piece."

"It isn't," she murmured. But she didn't want to correct him too much. By the sound of things, Forester was at least willing to give her the benefit of the doubt.

If the tube she'd tossed into the bushes had wedged in the branches... then that meant perhaps whoever had come along after her to plant it had done so without finding the tube. Perhaps they'd intended to but failed.

A stroke of luck, then. At least enough of a stroke that Forester wasn't currently hauling her off in cuffs. She did notice that neither Wade nor

Grant were nearby. The rule-bending, sociopathic, ex-fighter was one thing, but the other two?

No—this was the limit to the help she would get. Artemis knew that much.

Jamie's hand was still rigid, causing her heart to ache. She didn't say anything, but she took a step away until his hand fell. She was waving towards the tube.

"Pictures of the Ghost-killer?" she asked.

"That's right." Forester nodded once.

"So..." Artemis glanced between Jamie and Cameron, "if they didn't lift my fingerprints from that tube... then where?"

Jamie shrugged. "Your apartment?"

"No," she said quickly. "I have my own camera. No one has been over."

Except for you, she thought. But she didn't dare voice this out loud. Jamie was on her side. She knew it. She refused to even consider the alternative.

She also couldn't consider things with Tommy's strange note, his apparition of Helen, or otherwise, and the way the Professor was involved in all of it.

"So," Artemis said, tapping her fingers against her thigh and beginning to pace. Her cheeks felt moist. The air brushed against her skin.

"Assuming you two believe I didn't kill a man in cold blood, we only have one option."

"It's not the video footage," Forester said.

"No. I believe you. So if not the footage, that means the security camera picked up something *real*. An actual interaction with someone... It *had* to have been *after* I left."

"How so?" Forester said.

"I need that footage," Artemis murmured.

"Fair, but how so?" Forester pressed.

"Because," she retorted, "It's an old mentalism trick. I could do a much smaller variety with three pieces of paper. On one of the papers, I simply write the word tails."

"Tails?"

Artemis nodded. "And then, I hide what I've written. It goes like this. First, I waffle a bit. I tell you that I've come up with your dream for the future. I then write down *tails* and ask you—what is your dream?" She pointed at Forester. "You might hesitate. Think I'll cheat. So I'll prove that I've locked in my written answer. I'll hide it under a glass. No way to get at it. Relieved, you'll tell me you one day want to be an ice-skater in Paris."

"You know me so well," Forester said, wiggling his eyebrows.

"Perhaps," she retorted. "But then I'll move on to a *second* piece of paper. The whole thing is designed to convince you that I can read your mind. A complete sham, but I ask a *second* question. Say, what's your favorite childhood memory. I dramatize it. I get emotions involved. The subconscious is my ally in this."

Artemis pretended as if she was slipping another piece of paper beneath an imaginary glass. "See, now? I ask you what your favorite memory is. But when I write down my answer... I don't write down a memory. I write down *ballet, in Paris.* Then I slide it under the cup. I've answered the *first* question with my *second* guess. You don't know I'm cheating. You assume I've guessed fairly and put both under. So you tell me your favorite childhood memory, thinking there's no way I've guessed it. And you'd be right. You tell me..." Artemis wiggled her hand in a sort of circle in the air.

Forester helped out by murmuring, "The time I took my mom to the hospital..." He wasn't smiling, wasn't teasing.

Artemis glanced at him but didn't comment, continuing, "Alright. So your favorite childhood memory is a trip with your mother to a hospital. And that's when I ask the third question. Heads or tails. I use a false coin. Both sides tails. The person is so conditioned to think that they're getting a fair choice, they make a guess. Heads, let's say. I flip the fake coin. We get tails. And I say, I guess I now must write *tails* down."

Forester clicked his tongue. "But instead, for your final guess... you write down *hospital, mother.* Something like?"

"Exactly," Artemis said, pointing at him. "That way, I've answered all three questions correctly. Just out of order. I answered tails first. And then I skipped each *actual* guess to write down the answer of the previous question."

"I think I'm confused," Jamie said.

Artemis nodded. "It's a Ponzi scheme. That's what the video is. It's the only option."

Forester was nodding now, his eyes brightening. He looked impressed. "So you're saying Azin had a conversation with you, you left—"

"Yes. And then, given the time crunch, *immediately* afterwards, he did the whole thing. Staged it all. With a woman who looked a bit like me. She must have had a wig, contact lenses. Something similar."

Forester tapped his foot. "What about the sweater?"

"Pardon?"

"She was wearing the same sweater you had."

Artemis shook her head, feeling a faint chill. "Then..." she bit her lip. "She must have been following me. The woman in the second video."

"Wait, *second* video?" Jamie asked.

"The one recorded after I left," Artemis said, feeling her confidence growing as she said it. The process of elimination only gave one option. She had *not* killed Azin. The footage hadn't been doctored. The video was real. And the video was necessarily taken *after* her interaction with

Azin, in order to allow her own words to be used against her. The gun was planted *after* the footage of her throwing the photos into the bushes. Improvisation? Perhaps. Regardless... It was the only thing that made sense.

"They recorded a second video," Jamie said slowly. "In order to frame you? But that means..."

"Azin was in on it," Artemis said. "He must have been. And then *she,* whoever she is, killed him for real."

"Maybe someone paid her," Forester said slowly. "I noticed something open on Ross Dawkins' desk as I left the sheriff's department."

"Oh?"

"Mhmm. Ads for high-end prostitutes."

Jamie snorted. "Probably more of a personal vice than anything to do with this. Ross isn't exactly a... churchgoing man."

Forester nodded, but said, "He'd circled all the brunettes."

Artemis glanced at him. The agent just shrugged.

"Do you know their numbers?" she said quickly.

Forester snorted. He tapped a finger to his forehead. "Not all of us have that psychic memory thing of yours, Checkers."

Artemis shook her head, stomping a foot and trying to dislodge both the cold and some numbness. She said, "Well... if the Dawkins family is behind it, then Ross would make a good go between. Maybe they hired a prostitute to play my part. Then they may have used her, threatened her, to kill Azin. Maybe she didn't even know there were bullets in the gun." Artemis was nodding now, excitedly. "In fact, if anyone could register a weapon in my name in Pinelake' it's the Dawkins family. A family of cops. They'd have perfect access."

"Fingerprints?" Forester asked.

She sighed. "I mean... a month ago they tried to arrest me. Maybe then? Or just some PI... maybe the taxi driver. I don't know."

"Fine, we'll figure out the fingerprints later," said Forester. "So our working theory is someone went to the effort of framing you by staging a miniature, drama production in the window of time since you left Azin's but before he died."

"Yes," Artemis said firmly. "It's the only thing I can think of."

Forester shrugged, glancing at Jamie. "You wanna put on your big boy pants and help out, or you gonna play house on the prairie some more?"

"Hey!" Artemis said. "Be nice."

Jamie, though, stepped forward. He held a hand against her, again, as if claiming his territory. He scowled at Forester. "Some of us have responsibilities. We don't spend our lives acting like we're twelve."

"Yeah—I saw you at the party. You seemed to like twelve-year-olds."

"That's my sister, you piece of—"

"Cameron!" Artemis snapped.

Forester raised his hands, chuckling wolfishly and shaking his head. There wasn't an ounce of remorse as his cold gaze met Jamie's. "Just a joke," Forester drawled. He winked. "Lighten up, big guy. Imma save your girlfriend's ass. And it's a nice ass—*trust* me." Then, before Artemis could yell again or before Jamie could shout, Forester turned, strolling lazily towards his car. He only paused in the door long enough to glance back. And, for the briefest moment, Artemis thought she spotted a glimpse of pain in his eyes as he looked where Artemis and Jamie stood near each other.

He covered with a little snort of derision and then gestured. "You'd better come with me, Checkers. If we're gonna stop by a dirty cop's place, you're gonna want firepower."

"Go to hell!" Jamie shouted. "Get out of here. She doesn't want anything to do with you..." He trailed off though, glancing down where Artemis was touching his arm. She winced at him and gave a shake of her head. "It's awful," she murmured. "I know it's awful. He's awful... well, not always." She shot an angry look at where the sociopath had slipped back into the front seat of the car. He'd turned his high-beams on, spotlighting the two of them.

"He's a petty jackass," Jamie snarled, turning to look away from the glare. "You can't seriously want to go with him."

"I don't *want* to. I have to. Please understand. He's right—I need firepower. I need to find out if the Dawkins were behind all of this. Even if I'm right, no judge will believe me without proof."

"Of course, you're right," Jamie said firmly. But again, his hand was tense, and again it hurt, and again she couldn't blame him.

"Please, Jamie... I'll figure this out. We can spend the weekend on the ranch. I dunno, do something fun. With Sophie. Or not. Whatever you want."

Jamie swallowed, standing in the cold mist. He'd come all this way for her. Risked his own life, his own freedom for her. And it felt like a betrayal to walk away from him, to go sit in that car with Agent Forester.

Cameron was behaving like a right ass. She made a mental note to slap him when all of this was over. "You don't deserve that," she said quietly.

"What did he mean about that last part?"

"Which one?"

"He said you had a nice..." Jamie blushed, clearing his throat. "Have you two—"

"No!" she protested quickly, her cheeks reddening. "No—not at all. Yuck—with Cameron? No—hell no."

Jamie frowned. "That's a lot of no's."

"Because there's not a chance," she said quickly. "I swear, we haven't."

"He's good-looking," Jamie said slowly, shifting where he stood.

Artemis frowned. "I don't know how to respond to that. He's fine. But you saw—he's a psycho. Just... for now... he's a psycho on my side. And I need him."

This last part set Jamie's jaw clenching. He closed his eyes, exhaled briefly, then said, quietly, "I know... I know... I'm sorry. I don't mean to make it difficult. I just..." he opened his eyes and forced a quick smile. The kindness, though, had already reached his eyes, softening them. "I don't want to... to lose you again. I don't think I could take another loss ."

Artemis looked Jamie dead in the eyes. The lights from Forester's car illuminated the two of them. She wanted to say something to make it feel better.

But the only thing she could think to do didn't involve words.

She leaned in, quick, absolutely indifferent and simultaneously entirely aware of their audience. She kissed Jamie. A long, aggressive kiss. He'd been holding her, touching her—claiming his territory. And now it was her turn.

He hesitated for only a second in surprise. But then eagerly, with equal hunger, he met her lips with his. Their mouths were cold at first, but their shared body heat warmed them. His lips were soft like she remembered, and he smelled of aftershave from the party. She smelled of soap—she didn't tend to use perfume.

He cradled her head, and her eyes closed.

For a moment, she forgot the rest of it. Forgot about Helen, Tommy, the Professor, her father, forgot about the murder charges, Azin's death... All of it.

She remembered two things.

Jamie Kramer.

And the audience. If Cameron thought he could talk like that, treat Jamie like that, then she hoped in whatever small, shriveled, turnip-of-a-heart he had watching their kiss was deeply painful. She wouldn't allow herself to consider *why* that might be.

But her subconscious knew why she'd chosen to kiss Jamie. And all three of them near the pond knew why Jamie was all too delighted to kiss her back.

It felt like victory when the high beams on Forester's car faded, and Jamie and Artemis were cast in darkness.

As this happened, Jamie held her a moment longer and then released her to draw air, giggling as he did. He whispered in her ear, "Bet he didn't like that."

Artemis just shook her head. She didn't want to get into another discussion about Cameron. "Are we good?" she whispered, pressing her forehead against his chest briefly, enjoying his warmth.

Jamie kissed her forehead. "Yeah. Definitely."

She looked up, smiling at him, and winked.

"Be safe," he said. His smile was gone. "Please."

"Promise," she replied. "You too. Where's Sophie, by the way?"

"The Washingtons are staying at the ranch for a bit. Watching her."

Artemis winced, remembering her friends. "Okay... well... don't tell them you saw me, alright? It will only put you in danger. If Agent Butcher finds out—"

The horn to Forester's car started blaring, piercing the night in loud shrieks.

Jamie growled, half-turning, his hand bunched. Artemis caught him, remembering the last time Jamie had tried to strike Forester. It had ended with Jamie eating dirt and Forester barely noticing anything had happened.

The two men couldn't have been more different. Jamie was safety, solace, peace and warmth. A warm fire, comfort.

Forester was a jackass, blaring his horn. A dangerous jackass... A very dangerous jackass. Then again... he'd saved her life on more than one occasion.

She swallowed, winced apologetically, and gave Jamie another quick peck for good measure, then headed towards the vehicle, scowling as she approached. She picked up her pace when she reached the parking lot, hastening towards Forester's car and pausing only once to glance back to where Jamie stood on the path watching her.

CHAPTER TEN

THE DRIVE HAD PASSED in relative silence. Under the cover of dark, most of the roads lying empty in the dead of night. Artemis had tried to hold her tongue as Forester guided them towards Ross Dawkins' home, but as they turned off a main road onto a side street, she couldn't help but break the uncomfortable silence.

"What the hell was that?"

"Hmm? A house. Not his—Ross's is that big one... Oh, wait, nope. Two more streets."

Artemis glared at Forester's lumpy ear. She resisted the urge to flick it. "You're not funny. And you're not clever. Why did you treat Jamie like that? He's my friend. He was *helping*!"

Forester pulled the car suddenly to the side of the road, turned off the engine, locked the doors and looked at her.

"What?" she snapped.

He said, "Oh, nothing. Just thought I was risking my career, my life, everything for you. You know. No big deal. But I said some mean words to poor little Jamie Kramer and suddenly I'm the big bad wolf. Which I guess makes you Little Red Riding Hood. I'll make sure to keep an eye out if I ever see you with granny's shotgun."

"What? You know what, never mind. Forester, I *appreciate* you helping. Now keep driving."

"Which is it, Checkers?" he said, eyes hooded again, head leaning back casually, fingers drumming the steering wheel. "You wanna talk about our feelings, or do you want me to save your ass?"

"How about, for a start, you stop commenting on my ass."

Forester glanced at her, again flashing something lupine in his gaze. "I'm not a tame puppy, Artemis. But you know that. That's why you were gonna call me. It's why your brother *did* call me. You don't need a tame puppy for this. So how about you stop worrying about the big ol' beast peeing on the carpet or ripping a couple of throw pillows, and focus on the fact that he ripped the neck out of an intruder while little Spud trembled in his kennel."

"I—what? Spud? Forester, this might be a difficult concept for you to grasp. But let me try—and I'll speak slow, with small words to help. Does that sound alright?"

"Smart lady say what?"

"You can *do* more than one thing at the same time. Shocker, I know. For one, you can help. Which I appreciate. But, hold on, here's the complicated part," she said, making no attempt to keep the sting from her voice. "You can *also* not be a piece of shit to my boyfriend."

"Ha! Boyfriend? Is that it?"

Artemis felt her cheeks flush at this. Quickly, to cover for her sudden embarrassment, she said, "Another example of being able to do two things is talking *and* driving. So how about you start the engine and let's go to Dawkins'."

To her surprise, Forester complied. He started the car, pulled away from the curb and began moving slowly back towards Ross' house. As he did, they passed larger and larger mansions, crowded together on small quarter-acres. Sprawling patios and decks competed with one another for dominance.

Forester stared through the windshield, blinking a couple of times as he did. He was breathing heavily, and for a moment, Artemis was worried he might lose it.

This was not a safe man. And perhaps he was right—perhaps that was *exactly* why he was the one here helping.

When he glanced at her, though, he spoke quietly, with less mockery and scorn behind every sentence. Instead, he said crisply, "You're right, Ms. Blythe. Maybe I did behave somewhat recklessly. Congratulations to you and Kramer. Henceforth," he added, raising his hand and holding it in a mock salute, "I shall *not* comment on your magnificent posterior. Your callipygian form. Your—" He caught himself, cleared his throat again, then grumbled, "Meant it as a compliment, by the way." He shook his head, looking through the glass once more.

Artemis just sighed, shaking her head. "You're not the only one with a hard life, Cameron," she murmured, staring out the window at the moon. She was just too exhausted to engage with him.

It was surprising, then, when a faint muttered comment caught her ear. She barely heard it, as if he'd said it while clearing his throat.

"Sorry..."

She glanced over, but he was staring determinedly through the windshield. Then, before she could say anything, he pointed. "Ah—there we are. Mr. Rossy's big ol' abode. Huh, speaking of dogs."

He trailed off, still pointing, and Artemis followed his indicating finger to spot glaring yellow eyes peering through slits in a black fence. Their car trundled to a halt outside the house. Artemis spotted a police cruiser parked in the driveway, next to a large minivan.

The house itself was gigantic—far larger than most police patrolmen could afford. Their grandfather's money, most likely. He'd been sheriff for decades now and had more than his fair share of campaign donors.

"Cameras?" Artemis said, realizing she'd likely be keeping an eye out for recording devices the rest of her life.

"Yeah, couple. See the glint? There—porch. There, screen door. There, front door."

Artemis followed his quick motions. Now that they had arrived, Forester was cool and collected again. Eyes hooded, attention directed at the problem to be solved.

Artemis calmed herself, refocusing her attention. The problem in the car wasn't the main threat right now. She refused to glance in Cameron's direction, preferring now to study the tall chain-link fence blockading Ross Dawkins' garden. The hounds were not bellowing yet, but their eyes glowed in the dark, threatening all comers.

Artemis swallowed faintly. She murmured, "Any ideas?"

Before she'd even finished, Forester was already shoving out of the vehicle. He eased the door shut and then, with lanky strides, crossed the front yard, circling around the other side of the house towards where no dogs were visible.

The hounds, however, seemed to sense the deception. One of them began to growl. The other turned, revealing a clipped tail nub, and scampered off into the grass, suggesting he was likely circling the house to confront Forester's new trajectory.

Artemis hissed beneath her breath. She wished the man would have given her at least a few seconds to strategize.

But he was already moving again, his fingers through the chain link as he began to scale the fence. "Forester!" she hissed through the open window.

He, quite predictably, ignored her.

She cursed, pushed out of the car, eased the door shut as quietly as possible, did her best not to glance in the direction of the watchful hound waiting by the left-side gate, and hurried towards the right side of the large, brick home. She passed under a jutting terrace, grateful for the embrace of shadows, and arrived at Forester's side.

He was straddling the top of the gate now, glancing towards another row of cameras along the side of the house. "Paranoid thumb-head, isn't he?" Forester said, swinging his legs like a child on a teeter-totter.

"Forester," Artemis whispered. "Careful. Dog."

The second hound had indeed circled the house and was now sitting in the grass within spitting distance of Forester, watching the man and growling in its throat.

"Huh, not barking," Forester said.

But Artemis could hear *why* the creature wasn't braying. The growl was a graveling, painful sound, suggesting that Ross had snipped his animals' vocal chords. The same way he had snipped their tails.

She found her disdain for the youngest Dawkins brother only increasing.

Granted, the fact that he'd tried to attack her tonight only further increased her anger with him. The dog sat in the grass, paws digging into the grassy terrain, the painful growl humming like one of Tommy's motorbikes.

Forester was ignoring the animal, though. Instead, the big man had stretched to his full height, balancing on the top of the gate and reaching for a small window on the second floor.

"Forester," she whispered. "Careful!"

Cameron paused and followed her indicating finger. Artemis had avoided the cameras up to this point, sticking to the shadow beneath the terrace and now hugging the brick facade. But Forester was dangerously close to showing himself. In fact, one of his arms, by the look of things, had already strayed into view of one of the house's side-facing surveillance devices.

Artemis hoped that none of his distinguishing tattoos or scars had been visible. Forester lowered his hand quickly when he spotted the reflection of the glass.

"Oh, shit," he muttered. "Huh... Maybe if I..." he began to lower himself into the garden, on the side of the dogs, clearly aiming towards a small, cellar door which was out of camera view.

The moment his leg dropped, though, the growling hound snarled, flashing teeth and darting forward.

Forester jerked his leg back up in the nick of time as the rottweiler tried to rip his foot clean off. The metal fence shook and rattled as the dog's hundred plus pound frame slammed into the gate. Forester wobbled precariously in his position, and Artemis darted out, pushing up against his waist to keep him from falling.

Forester settled and gave her a quick nod of gratitude. Then, he pointed off into the garden, clicking his fingers. "Hey, Checkers," he whispered. "Hand me a rock."

"What?"

"Rock. There."

She did as he asked, snatching a hefty stone from beneath the terrace and handing it to Cameron. He then leaned back, tossing the rock a couple of times—nearly dropping it—cursing, steadying and then taking aim.

"What are you—" she began.

And he launched the stone, aiming at the camera facing the second-floor window above the fence. The stone struck the side of the camera, knocking it a couple of inches to the right.

"Huh," Forester said. "Good stuff. I was trying to shatter it, but that works too."

Artemis winced but decided he was right. The camera was no longer facing the second-floor window. Forester now clambered up the side of the house, hands latching onto the windowsill, and then he jammed his fingers against the base of the window.

"People," he muttered, gasping in exertion, "never..." He wiggled his thumb, his legs dangling and feet kicking against the brick. "—lock second floor windows." He gasped in delight as the window slid a bit and shot a look over his shoulder at her, beaming merrily.

She just shrugged. He kicked his legs, arms straining, and he pulled himself through the gap in the second floor window, disappearing from view with another kick.

Now the dog's eyes landed on Artemis. The second hound had arrived from the left side of the house, also glaring at Artemis, also growling.

"Good puppy," she whispered.

They both snarled. In a way, the rottweilers very much reminded her of their owner. She stared at the fence, back at the window. Forester's scarred hand was jutting through, waving at her and gesturing for her to join him.

She swallowed, trying to keep her fear at bay.

As much experience as she now had stumbling through dangerous places, often filled with creepy things, it hadn't become any easier. She could feel the knot forming in her stomach. Could feel her fear crawling along her spine like some many-legged thing.

She wanted to turn, to run back to the car and disappear.

Seeing that scarred and disembodied hand wave at her only further exacerbated her terror.

It was a testament to the desperation of the moment that the only ally she had within earshot was Cameron Forester. At any other time, this thought might have completely discouraged her.

There was no telling what Forester would do.

Then again...

She was asking him to help her break into a local policeman's private residence in search of evidence that he'd framed her for murder... And likely Ross had returned home at this point. She'd been far enough away for long enough with Tommy. It wasn't like Dawkins would've just lingered for two hours waiting to get busted for accosting a prisoner. Knowing Ross... he was probably home.

Which meant...

Unpredictable and outside-the lines was exactly what she needed. That was what Forester brought to the table.

She was stalling. She knew that.

Her mind would often do this when faced with a difficult task—an obvious attempt to avoid the inevitable. She had to climb that fence. Had to hope she didn't slip and turn into puppy chow. And she had to find a way through that second floor window.

Even as she tried to talk herself into it, her mind still protesting every step along the way, her stomach knotted some more.

"Just do it!" a voice whispered above. "Thinking makes it worse."

"Thinking makes it worse," she muttered darkly to herself. If ever there was a phrase that perfectly suited a man of Cameron's temperament, it was this. She snorted and then tentatively approached the gate.

She pushed her fingers through the mesh. One of the dogs tried to rip them off. Lunging and snarling. She yanked her hand back, slobber speckling her knuckles, teeth grazing her skin.

She yelped and shook her hand, eyes widened in panic.

Forester peeked his head back through the window. "Sometime tonight, Checks?"

She glared at him. "Please *do not* truncate the already insulting nickname."

"My bad," he muttered, both hands shooting out through the window on either side of him as if offering surrender. "What's the hold-up?"

She pointed at the dogs. "Hell hounds."

"I see... Climb quick?"

"I was trying that," she said crossly.

She approached the fence again, motivated by the sheer refusal to look weak in front of Cameron. She tried to hurry the process. Fingers through the fence. Foot finding a spot to push off. A quick lunge up.

But the dogs lunged again. She yelped, the fence rattled, and she stumbled back, this time certain her forefinger was bleeding. When she looked down, though, she spotted no injury.

Now, both hounds were pacing back and forth at the foot of the fence, growling at her, their yellow eyes like the glare of demons in the dark.

Then, suddenly behind her, Artemis heard the sound of an approaching vehicle. She froze. Cameron didn't move, just watching curiously where he'd jammed himself back out the window. He even gave a little mocking wave as a long, blue sedan pulled up the street, headlights flashing, and then continued along, disappearing up a side cul-de-sac.

Cameron was no longer waving. He glanced down at Artemis. "Wanna just wait out here?" he said.

"No need to sound so smug," she shot back.

He grinned. "You picked up on that? I was worried you might not."

"Ass."

"I thought we were forbidden from talking about those. I saw you checking me out, Checkers."

"Forester. Shut up."

He shrugged. Then he slipped back through the window, dangled down in a show of upper body strength, deposited himself back on the fence, took two steps across the top of the gate, perfectly balanced, and dropped to a sitting position on the opposite side of the gate. He dangled his feet again, if only to tease the dogs who were now lunging to try and snare his sneaker.

Forester chuckled as the hounds bounced off the metal fence. "I think I like them," he muttered. "They're feisty. Here, take my hand." He offered his scarred palm towards her.

Artemis stared at the extended arm. A small, petty part of her wanted to refuse. But that would be the sort of thing Cameron would do. She'd come here for a reason, and if it meant she needed a little bit of help climbing a gate, as embarrassing as it was, she would do what was needed.

And so, biting back any comment or pride, she reached out. He snagged her hand, gave a quick wink and then pulled her, in one smooth motion, bodily off the ground. He didn't even seem to strain. He deposited her on the edge of the gate. His hands found her waist, holding her briefly, trying to balance her so she wouldn't fall off.

As she felt his calloused hands against her ribs, she hesitated. There was something strangely *pleasant* about the touch of his fingers against her. The sheer strength of his hands holding her from falling off the—

She scowled, cutting off this train of thought. She pushed firmly at his hand, dislodging it. "I'm fine. Thank you," she added, coldly.

And then, she gestured towards the window. "You first."

"You worried I'm going to stare?"

"Forester, playful cheek and criminal harassment are separated only by the thin line of my good will. Are we clear?"

"Not really. Here, hold tight." Forester sidled past her. A difficult proposition, as they were balanced on a three inch piece of metal bar. She ducked as he hopped over her, his hands shooting out and catching against the brick work.

Then, like a monkey, he clambered back up the side of the building and through the window once more.

This time, he leaned out again, hand towards her.

And again, swallowing her pride, she accepted the offer. And again, he lifted her bodily, pulling her off the fence.

She figured in that moment, she looked like a much more bizarre version of Mary Poppins. Except instead of an umbrella, she had two hundred and twenty pounds of mean and muscle.

As she clambered through the window, Forester slid the glass shut behind her. The two of them crouched in the dark, by the window, both breathing quietly.

Both listening.

No sound from inside the house. Only the faint growling of the creatures in the garden.

"Hear anything?" Artemis whispered.

Forester paused, grunted. "Nah. We're good. So... remember, Dawkins was looking up brunette prostitutes. If we can get his phone or computer, we can see if he contacted any of them to set you up."

"Right." Artemis hesitated. "Also, any records for firearm purchases. To see if they registered a weapon in my name. A police department would have all the personal information, social security and the like needed."

Forester chuckled.

"What?"

"It's cute that you think you need all that for a gun."

"Things are tighter in this State, Cameron. It would take *a lot* of information for them to purchase a firearm registered in my name."

"Fair enough. So looking for whores and guns. Sounds like a Friday night. Split up or go together?"

Artemis considered this. In a way, she instinctively wanted to stick next to Cameron. He was serving as a security blanket. She hated how much safer she felt with him next to her. She couldn't imagine doing this on her own.

At calm seas, Forester was the threat. In storming oceans, he was the solution.

But she refused to rely on this. Refused, adamantly, to *need* him for simply emotional reasons. "Splitting up will cover more ground. If you find Ross's room, be careful."

"He lives alone, by the way," Forester replied. "His ex-wife bought a new house two years ago."

Artemis thought of the dogs with their snipped tails and vocal cords. Thought of the sound of Ross and his brother Merl sneaking towards her jail cell.

Her eyes narrowed. The thought of him living alone felt appropriate.

And it would certainly make it easier for them to move about unde-tected.

"Alright—I got the stairs. You want second floor?"

"Sure," she replied. "Be careful."

But he was moving already. He hopped the stair rail, dangled and released. A faint *thump* as he hit the first floor landing, leaving her alone in the dark by the window.

Now, she felt confident, Cameron was just showing off.

She shook her head in frustration, feeling a strange tingle along her ribs where he'd been holding her. And determinedly pretending as if she hadn't felt a thing, she straightened and began to move, heading towards one of the doors closest to her on the second floor.

Chapter Eleven

Artemis gave a final glance into the second room. Also empty. The walls bare. The bed missing. No furniture save a dresser, which Artemis had already combed through, finding nothing of interest.

She huffed in frustration. The first room—a bathroom. The second, an empty bedroom.

She peered down the hall at the third room. The door shut. Would Ross be sleeping on the second floor, or the first?

She hadn't heard any gunshots, or shouting from below, which suggested to her that Forester hadn't yet stumbled upon the corrupt cop either.

She moved along the hall, towards this third and final door, swallowing and pausing. She listened intently. A faint sound exuded from within, beyond the wooden frame. A low, rumbling sound. Not dissimilar to the growl of the dogs.

She touched the door handle.

Warmer than the other two had been.

Shit.

She exhaled slowly, shooting a quick glance down the stairs, peering into the dark landing. But Forester was nowhere to be seen; she was very much on her own. Artemis shifted uncomfortably from one foot to the other, the carpeting indenting beneath her.

And then, summoning her resolve, she twisted the handle and eased the door in. The hinges, mercifully, didn't creak. A newer house, suggesting the structure itself would whisper instead of warn.

She stepped onto a thicker, pale carpet in this room.

A bedroom.

Not just because of the bed she spotted against the wall. Nor simply due to the sound of snoring exuding from this bed, originating due to a lump under the covers.

But also because of the rank smell. Body odor, cigarettes and old pizza.

She spotted a couple of pizza boxes stacked on a small duvet tossed in the corner, beneath a cracked window. A fan whirred in the ceiling, perpetually stirring the noxious air of the bedroom. There was an en-suite bathroom, and judging by a quick glance into the space, she desperately hoped her search wouldn't lead her onto those streaked tiles. Even from where she stood, she thought she spotted wadded tissue in the sink.

Wrinkling her nose and holding back a visceral reaction of disgust, she took another tentative step into the room. A couple of discarded socks on the floor served as mines, which she deftly avoided. As she took another step forward, her stomach twisted again. This time, a powerful surge of anxiety accompanied the horrible sensation.

She found herself going still, staring at the lump beneath the bed. She glimpsed the man's shaved head. Watched the way his body moved with his breath, one arm extended up past his head at an odd angle, fingers draped against the headboard. She spotted an absolutely enormous hand gun resting on the nightstand by Ross's thick skull.

She stared at the weapon, trying to keep her breathing in check. She shot a look over her shoulder towards the door, which was slowly swinging shut, suggesting the angle of the room was slightly slanted. She resisted the desire to return and wedge the door.

Resisted, also, the urge to go fetch Forester. Perhaps he'd found something downstairs... a work laptop? Something?

Her eyes landed on the same nightstand which situated the *other* side of the bed from where she stood. A faint white tail in the form of a charging cable moved up from a wall outlet, plugged into...

There. His phone.

Dammit.

She would have to creep completely around the bed in order to reach the phone... she bit her lip, hoping the pain would help still her rising anxiety.

She held her own breath briefly, not just to avoid breathing what she felt confident was toxic air but also to listen.

Ross was still snoring, still breathing heavily. Still asleep.

Judging by the empty bottles on *this* side of the bed, it would take some doing to rouse the man. She could be quiet, couldn't she? She was small... She took another tiptoeing step into the room. Then another, and another, navigating the occasional pizza box or discarded, crumpled clothing item.

She rounded the edge of the bed, dread in her heart and realizing now that if she wasn't careful, and if Ross woke, he would be closer to the door than she was.

Not to mention, he likely wouldn't even attempt to chase her. That big old gun on his nightstand would puncture a hole in her spine so large they'd be able to pass a bowling ball through it.

Dark thoughts. Morbid thoughts.

And yet facing them allowed her another step.

Her fingers trailed along the wooden foot-board, knuckles brushing the smooth lacquer. As she stepped around the side of the large, king-sized bed, she nearly stepped on a hand.

Artemis went still, freezing in place.

She stared down.

The hand belonged to an arm which belonged to a woman.

At first, Artemis thought the woman was dead. Her mind cast back to the dreadful images she'd seen of her own father in bed with one of his victims... after he'd killed her.

She shuddered. She was glad to find that she didn't scream, didn't yell, but rather stared, her nostrils flaring as a breath escaped in a burst.

But then the woman moved. Only slightly, shifting from one arm to the next. Her dark hair stretched around her face like seaweed on the surf. The woman had very pleasant features, and Artemis frowned. Did the woman look like *her*?

No... Not at all. She was a beautiful woman but not the quiet pretty of Artemis' features. This woman, also, had a tattoo along the side of her neck. A curving tail in purple and pink, like that of a dragon swishing b y.

She studied the tattoo briefly, frozen at the foot of the bed, wondering if she'd seen that same tattoo on the video back in Azin's place...

But no. No, the woman in that video hadn't *had* a tattoo. Covered it then?

Perhaps. But this woman's hair was far lighter. Her features different. Still... movie magic? Artemis took a second to scan the woman up and down a final time... In the dark, it had been hard to tell. But now, as she leaned closer, she realized something...

This woman *definitely* hadn't been in the video. She had beautiful, olive skin. The woman in the video Artemis had watched had been pale alabaster like Artemis.

No. This was not the mysterious figure playing out the murder of Azin.

Which left a couple of questions... why was she wedged on the side of the bed next to Ross?

Artemis glanced about a bit more. The woman, she realized, had a blanket beneath her, serving as a makeshift mattress. She also had a pillow tucked under her head.

Artemis remembered what Forester had said about Ross perusing high-end escorts... Was this one of them?

Most likely. Artemis wrinkled her nose in disgust. Not at the woman but at the knowledge that the chances Ross had *paid* rather than manipulated for the woman's services were low at best. She could absolutely see the policeman using his badge in order to get what he wanted.

And he hadn't even seen the point in letting the woman sleep on the same bed as him. She was wedged against the wall, like a pet, kept on the floor to avoid shedding.

Artemis' eyes bounced from the woman on the ground back up to Ross's form. Now, on this side of the bed, she could make out his features.

Somehow, if possible, he looked even meaner while sleeping. This was attributable to the way that, with eyes closed and lips sealed, his head looked even more like a boulder than a human skull.

Artemis could imagine the thing dislodging on the side of a mountain, tumbling down, crashing through branches and boughs alike, indiscriminate.

As she stood there, her feet facing the woman wedged between the bed and the wall, glaring at the corrupt cop, she couldn't help but realize how the roles had reversed. This man had intended her harm. Had intended to creep into her cell, along with his brother, and do all manner of mischief. The idea that she would have survived the night was a far shot.

And now there she stood, with him at her temporary mercy. How hard would it be to snatch that gun and solve her Dawkins problem once and for all?

Even as she thought it, she felt a surge of horror and guilt.

Her palms felt sweaty, and she rubbed them against the side of her shirt. She wasn't like Forester. She refused to be like him. She wasn't like Ross.

The Professor, the Ghost-killer, they all thought of her as some sort of killer in training. As someone they could manipulate, play with, use. Somehow leveraging her mind, her skills, to their corrupt use.

She glared at Ross, wishing she could lecture him, scold him. To let him know that she had chosen to let him live. Like Saul and David in the Old Testament. Their family had not been a churchgoing sort, but she remembered that story at least. Though she couldn't quite recall why that story came to mind. She hesitated, considering it then shaking her head. Perhaps it was because she felt like the small, overlooked shepherd. And she found herself in a world of giants, intending her and those she loved harm.

But she did not have a slingshot. What she did have was information. And she needed more of it.

She stared at the phone. The woman on the ground covered most of the space between where Artemis stood and the nightstand.

The woman wasn't moving too much. Occasionally smacking her lips, shifting her head. But otherwise, her body stayed in place.

And Artemis decided to risk it.

She stepped forward, placing her foot next to the woman, stepping on a blanket, if only to aid in muffling her footsteps. She paused, then skipped forward with a longer stride, avoiding the bed and moving back to the left side, closer to the wall.

She winced, tottering as she nearly jammed her foot against the splayed fingers of the woman beneath her.

Artemis managed to catch herself against the wall, bracing.

Nothing happened. No sounds of alarm, no movement. The snoring from Ross continued, the quiet breathing from the woman on the ground followed.

And now Artemis was inches from the phone. And also the gun.

She shivered, throat tense. It wasn't an exaggeration, she didn't think, to believe there was no way she might have done something like this only a couple of months before. Facing fear had a funny way of normalizing it. Perhaps that was what they called courage.

Really, Artemis just felt scared in multiple directions, confused enough in her fear to stumble her way into bravery.

She reached out, fingers touching the device plugged into the wall. She unplugged it and carefully slipped the cold thing into her pocket. She winced as the screen lit up, though. The moment she had unplugged it, the bright digital clock glared.

And then, she heard a faint murmur. Her heart froze. Her pulse quickened. She stared down, eyes wide, and the woman was now moving, looking up, blinking hurriedly.

"Hello? Mr. Dawkins?" the woman said, softly. She had a heavy Spanish accent, noticeable even in those three short words. Another reason to suspect this was not the woman in the video.

Artemis froze, one foot braced against the leg of the small bedside table, the other angled towards the bed, nearly stepping on the woman's hand.

Artemis looked down, and there, between her legs, she spotted the woman blinking, tilting her head back, and staring up.

A very awkward, precarious position. Artemis winced, watching the woman. The figure on the ground stared back, eyes like spotlights.

Artemis just shook her head and held a finger to her lips.

She wanted to scream, wanted to run for it. But the moment she did that, Ross would wake. Artemis glanced towards the weapon on the nightstand but didn't make her move. For the moment, tentative silence reigned. The quiet stretched between them. And then, the woman on the ground glanced at Ross.

She was alert now and suddenly jerked back, sitting up and pulling her blankets close around her. She stared at Artemis. "Who are you?" she whispered. Her voice quiet, hoarse, like the snipped vocal chords of those rottweilers, suggesting Ross very much loathed anyone disturbing his sleep.

Artemis shot a look at Ross. Still sleeping.

Not for much longer, though, if this woman started to make noise.

For a brief second, Artemis considered lying. She considered her options, hesitated, opened her mouth. Perhaps she could pass herself as a friend. If this woman really was a prostitute, it was unlikely she knew too much about Ross Dawkins' personal life.

Then again, to someone like this, would it be a good thing to be friends with Ross? Or a detriment?

In the end, though, Artemis simply told the truth. It was often easier to settle with what one could actually remember. But also, watching that woman, the way she huddled against the wall in fear, blankets tight around her form, shivering and staring between Artemis and Ross as if trying to determine which was the greater threat, Artemis couldn't help but feel a pang of sympathy.

The sympathy prompted truth. "I think he's a bad man," Artemis said, in a ghost of a whisper. "And I intend to prove it."

The woman stared. Artemis flinched, preparing to run for it. She intended to knock the pistol off the bedside, hoping to buy herself some time to reach the door.

The woman, though, studied her, eyes bright in the dark.

And then, her only response was to pull her legs back, clearing a path for Artemis. Another glance towards where Ross slept, and this time, Artemis could see the disgust in the woman's eyes.

Artemis gave a quick nod of gratitude.

The woman didn't reply.

Artemis hastened around the edge of the bed, picking up her pace.

Up until this point, her luck had held strong. But all good things eventually came to an end. As she rounded the foot of the bed, moving quickly, the phone in her pocket suddenly began to buzz.

The stolen phone. Dawkins' phone. She cursed, fumbling with the device, trying to turn it off. The buzz continued, and then, suddenly, the phone began to ring. A merry little tune, chirping in the dark.

Artemis clapped a hand against her pocket, failing to turn the volume down, hoping, in that final instant to muffle the sound.

Was it an alarm? Was someone calling him this late at night?

Either way, it didn't matter. The woman wedged against the wall grimaced, returning the sympathy Artemis had experienced moments before. But Artemis's gaze was drawn to Ross Dawkins. The man was rising slowly, grunting, swallowing, and wiping sleep from his eyes with the back of his knuckles. He blinked a few times and then froze. He was staring straight at her. She stared back.

Ross rubbed his eyes again, as if certain he was imagining things.

"Mirabelle?" he muttered. But then he spotted the woman wedged against the wall, and his eyes darted back towards Artemis. She watched as recognition dawned. Watched as the sleep faded completely, and he realized what he was staring at. Then, the corrupt cop cursed, emitted a loud shout of rage and lurched towards the large weapon left on his nightstand.

Artemis didn't wait to find out what he intended to do with it. She broke into a sprint, lunging back through the open door, kicking a pizza box out of the way in her flight. But even as she fled, there was a sound like a cannon. A chunk of plaster erupted off the wall just over her right shoulder, speckling her face with chips of paint and drywall.

That hand cannon would've blown her head off completely.

"Come back here, bitch!" screamed the cop.

Artemis did no such thing, scampering towards the stairs now. "Forester!" she yelled. "RUN!" She took the stairs two at a time. Heard the sound of scampering feet above her. A thud, another loud *bang!*

The wall above her exploded. She ducked as she did, instinctively, rounding the stairs and wishing she could have jumped the whole thing like Forester had.

She heard desperate yelling. The sound of footsteps following close behind. Artemis skidded along a slick, tiled floor, then came a to a sudden stop, staring wide-eyed.

Forester was standing over a body.

She gaped. Forester winced.

She stared at the thin man on the ground wearing spectacles. Well, more accurately, wearing *half* of his spectacles. The other half had skittered across the floor and gleamed under a small chandelier. Forester massaged his knuckles, pointed. "Those sounds ain't fireworks, are they?"

"He dead?" she yelled, still moving quickly.

"No... napping on the couch—oh, shit!" Forester dove to the side along with Artemis. Another loud gunshot.

The door behind them shattered. And suddenly, an alarm started chirping.

"Well, there goes that," Forester muttered. He had knocked Artemis into a side room—the living room judging by the table's and chairs with upholstery. Dawkins was snarling now. "Come here, little whore. I've been waiting for this for a *very* long time!"

Artemis tried to creep along the side of the wall, moving towards a second exit, opposite the one they'd arrived in. This second open doorframe looked as if it led into a kitchen which had a door leading into the side alley by the look of things—a straight shot. The alarm was still chirping, and Artemis didn't doubt any cops currently on duty were hurtling towards the house of one of their own.

But as she scampered forward, towards the kitchen, a figure suddenly appeared. She yelled.

Ross' hulking form stood in the door, his beer belly bare as he stood shirtless and hairy, in his boxers, glaring wide. He lifted his weapon, settling his stance from where he'd managed to cut around the side of the room.

Artemis tried to stumble back, but she couldn't outrun bullets.

Thankfully, Ross couldn't outrun chairs.

Forester flung one, and it caught the man in the face. The gunshot went wide and the weapon hit the ground, skittering.

Forester strolled forward now, whistling as he did, as if he had all the time in the world.

"Cam!" Artemis yelled desperately.

Forester hopped the toppled chair and gave a little flick of his foot, kicking the gun out of sight under the table.

Dawkins was groaning, rising to his feet. "Huh," Forester said. "Remember me? Probably best you don't, to be honest." And then

Cameron kicked the fallen cop hard. The man on the ground grunted, doubling over and letting out a loud whoosh of air.

Forester skipped over the man, to his other side now, almost as if he wanted to avoid giving Dawkins *too* long of a look. He bent down for a moment, lips lower, whispering in Dawkins' ear.

The cop on the ground groaned, trying to push up, bleeding from his nose and above his eye where Forester had pegged him with the chair.

Artemis didn't hear the first part of what Forester said, but faintly, she picked out the whisper—even as her own blood rushed through her system. "...don't like most people," Forester was whispering, his lips brushing Dawkins' ear. "But her?" he clicked his tongue. And suddenly, the whistling, the would-be humor, was all gone. Drained dry like sand from an hourglass.

All that remained in Forester's tone, in his eyes, was emptiness. A cold hollow.

It sent shivers up Artemis' arms as she steadied herself, trying to move around the table again, avoiding the gun on the ground.

There was something reptilian in Forester's eyes. He whispered, soft and crooning, "I lost her once to a man like you. I found that man. I did things..." Forester's whisper dropped even lower. "Things not even the devil's angels would repeat. Understand me, Ross? You don't have to be afraid of her. You don't have to be afraid of death. No... if you try to touch her again. *Ever.* I'll do things to you so creative they'll dedicate books to each piece I leave behind." Forester's hand patted the man on the ground. He straightened, adjusted his sleeves, smiled at Artemis and winked. Then raised his heel and football-kicked Dawkins in the back of the head.

A sound like *thwump*. Dawkins' face ricocheted off the door jam, and he went still.

Forester was still smiling that crocodile leer, as if he'd just had a mild conversation about the weather. He extended a hand in a gallant, little, sweeping gesture towards Artemis, as if to help her over the fallen figure.

But she didn't take that hand. She just stared, trembling. In that moment, she wasn't sure who scared her more. The cop who'd tried to kill her that night. Or the sociopath who'd protected her.

She swallowed, avoiding his fingers, and then she turned and sprinted in the opposite direction.

Running, running.

Fleeing Forester. Fleeing Ross.

Fleeing the whole damn thing.

This was too much. Far, far too much. She was a chess master. A woman who played a damn *game* for a living. This was just too much.

In the distance, she thought she could hear sirens, but she didn't care. She twisted the bolt on the large, front door. Shoved through, scampering out into the dark. Keeping her head low, in case anyone was watching, she sprinted towards the car.

On autopilot, she slipped into the front seat, turned the key where Forester had left it. Headlights glared. The engine came to life. And she sped away, peeling from the curb and racing back up the street.

Only after two streets did she realize she'd left Forester behind.

She'd *known* that was what she'd been doing. But not in a rational way. Emotionally, she'd wanted to distance herself. Rationally, she'd been frozen in place, watching that horrible image of Forester kicking Dawkins. That sickly, dull sound of foot connecting to skull.

Those whispered, terrible threats.

Forester didn't look at her the same way he did others. He didn't look at her how he had Dawkins. Somehow... Forester thought it was his job to... to...

She didn't even know.

"I lost her once to a man like you. I found that man. I did things... Not even the devil's angels would repeat."

She shuddered, briefly considering if she ought to go back. But Forester could take care of himself. He'd proven as much.

She didn't want to spend another second anywhere he could see her.

She couldn't. She'd *known* Forester was a monster. Known he was a man without a conscience who had done things to people that couldn't be repeated. She'd always thought he was a *tame* monster, though. It wasn't his actions, but his tone... that *cold hollow* that convinced her, irreversibly, otherwise.

She chuckled bitterly, flooring the gas, speeding away and back onto a highway. Off in the distance, in the rearview mirror, she spotted flashing lights speeding towards the side street she'd just taken.

They didn't follow her, though. As she raced along the highway away from Ross' home, she watched as the police cars veered onto the street that led to Dawkins' house.

She'd left Forester behind.

A man who'd helped her. A man who'd... saved her life. More than once. Again tonight.

And she'd left him.

Did that make her evil? Did it make her petty and cruel?

She feared so.

And yet she didn't turn the car. If anything, she pushed the pedal as far as it would go, speeding, speeding away.

She didn't think about breaking the speed limit. Didn't consider that a cop might pull her over for this alone.

That part of her mind wasn't functioning. She didn't even remember the phone she'd stolen, in her pocket now.

All she could think was to get as far away as she could.

CHAPTER TWELVE

Artemis sat on the side of the road, facing Pinelake's namesake. The water swished against the pine-needle strewn shore, taking some of its foliage-laden burden back out into the depths in teasing ripples.

Artemis' breath came in rapid puffs. The skies were clear, and the moon reflected in blue and yellow off the surface of the enormous lake. Her gaze traced the trees to a jutting, peninsular appendage of the coast, and then faltered. Many more acres of lake continued past this protrusion, but the waters were hidden from her gaze.

Artemis stared across the liquid, her heart tight in her chest as she returned her attention to the task at hand.

She hadn't heard from Forester, and now that her emotions had settled, her sense of guilt for leaving him behind had reached a crescendo.

Knowing Forester, though, he had probably beaten some hasty retreat, laughing while stealing some cop car.

At least, that's the story she had to tell herself to suppress her rising sense of guilt. She glanced back at the phone in her hand. The background image was of a skimpily clad bikini model winking coyly from the screen and using two beer bottles to cover her ample, silicone-inflated chest.

Artemis rolled her eyes. Some men were mysteries, difficult to place. Others, like Ross Dawkins, were as subtle as an elephant in a phone booth.

She tried to swipe up on the phone.

No luck. A four character pass-code.

She frowned, thinking slowly. Then, she entered Ross' name. It seemed likely, given the man. But the phone vibrated.

She tried his brother's name. Merl. At least their father had kept things to four letters—she wasn't sure Ross could count higher than that.

Again, the phone shook.

Then, her thumb accidentally entered two digits. The phone shook again.

"Shit, no!"

But her protest didn't matter. Now, the device warned her that she had five attempts left before it would lock her out. She seethed, glaring at the phone then glancing up once again to watch the lake.

She hesitated... then tried *lake.*

"No, no, stupid," she said even as she hit enter.

Again, another vibration.

"Think," Artemis murmured. Though, for Ross' pass-code, this advice might very well have been the worst sort. She considered for a moment. Thinking of Ross' family. His birthday... Did she know Ross' birthday?

She paused a moment, biting her lip. He'd been in school with her brother. She knew his birth *year*. She tried again. Nothing.

"Dammit," she seethed. If the phone locked her out, then all her efforts would have been for nothing.

"Huh," she muttered sarcastically. "Imagine if you had an FBI agent. He might be able to crack a phone. Who would've thunk it, Artemis? So smart. *Genius*." She shook her head scornfully and tried Ross' graduation year.

Two attempts left.

She tapped her fingers against her leg, considering Ross' threats to her. He'd shot first, asked questions later. He'd wanted to hurt her in the prison cell. He'd tried to assault her back outside the lake, a couple of cases ago.

Ross hated her guts. *Blythe*? No. Too many letters. Otto? Possibly... but no. The man wouldn't use the name of his grandmother's killer as a passcode.

But then Artemis went still. Eyebrows rising. She hesitated only a moment. Then, she fished out her own borrowed phone Jamie had provided. She quickly typed in one of the many memorized articles she had pertaining to her father's case.

It took some time for the old article, uploaded digitally, to load. But then she read through it, searching for... *there.*

Sharon Dawkins. Married to Abraham Dawkins. Born December 12th, 1941. She didn't read further, didn't want to remember how she'd been killed then found. How long it had taken for them to realize Otto Blythe was the culprit. Didn't want to remember her part in all of it. Calling in, correcting a simple mistake on the news station.

The wrong car. They'd identified the wrong car. She thought she'd been helpful at the time. She hadn't realized she'd been collapsing her life around her small shoulders.

But Artemis tried another passcode. 1941. The birth year of the woman who her father had killed. Ross' grandmother and the reason he loathed Artemis.

The phone vibrated.

Before her frustration could take hold, and as she stared at the final number, one remaining, warning her she was about to be locked out, she typed in the birth day and month. 1212.

The phone didn't vibrate. She stared.

She was in.

The screen changed. Another scantily clad desktop model. Artemis ignored this, feeling her fingers buzzing in excitement as she swept through the phone. She started with the most recent calls, cycling. She specifically checked calls placed the previous day. But as she read them, her excitement diminished somewhat.

The contacts were all stored.

Names like *Merl, Dad, Grandpa, AA.*

She paused, calling the last one. After one ring, she got a voicemail box from some Catholic church group hosting Alcoholics Anonymous. Artemis felt a little bit of her hatred for Ross diminish to something like a glimmer of respect.

At least the man was trying to fix himself.

But remembering the sound of his hushed voice outside of her cell quickly robbed her of any sense of charity.

She scanned through the other phone calls. But they were mostly accounted for. Artemis hesitated but then quickly swiped to the email tab at the bottom of the phone. She clicked, watching as the emails opened. She scanned the trash and spam folders. Then checked the inbox. At least six different ads for erectile dysfunction, more than one correspondence with an online sex-worker. But as Artemis scanned through the exchanged messages, she only felt nauseous.

Nothing to do with her. Or Azin. And none of the messages were sent last night.

Artemis drummed his phone against her leg, feeling a jolt of frustration. Ross Dawkins' phone was empty. No phone calls to Azin. None to some unknown number... unless he'd logged the suspicious number as a familiar name...

She considered this for a moment. She leaned back, though, exhaling in frustration.

She needed Forester. She knew she shouldn't have abandoned him, and now it was coming back to bite her.

She paused a second longer, frowning in consideration. She scanned the phone numbers once more, the email again. Nothing. The internet browser had been mostly used for the expected things on Ross' phone. None of them G-rated.

She shook her head in frustration. What she *didn't* see was any collusion. Any emails to his family about a plan to frame Artemis. She cycled to his Qwikpay app. No big transactions recently.

Nothing.

She was now resisting the urge to slam the phone against the dash. She scrolled back to the phone numbers, determined now. There—two calls to Merl around the time of Artemis' meeting with Azin. Perhaps Merl had been in on it... Or maybe it was a false name stored in his phone.

Artemis' fingers hovered over the name, on the verge of throwing caution to the wind... They could track this phone, though. If Ross told them she'd taken it.

If he could still tell anyone anything.

Thwump.

She winced against the echoing sound of Forester's foot catching the man's skull. She shifted uncomfortably. Then, instead of dialing Merl's number, she scrolled down, hastily, scanning how many times Ross had contacted his brother and partner. If this was a fake number, then there wouldn't be phone calls from months before.

But as she scrolled down, she spotted many of these calls, some around the same time, some with gaps for days, but all of them corresponding to the same number. A local area code, too.

And though she hated to admit it, she was finding it very difficult to think that this number belonged to anyone but Ross's brother.

And again, no communication with him. She skipped to the text messages. And again, besides the occasional exchange of inappropriate pictures or crude videos, there wasn't much substance to be found.

Which meant, horror of horrors, Ross Dawkins was not the orchestrator of all of this.

Of course, she had known from the beginning it was unlikely that Ross had planned anything; the man, by the look of him, couldn't plan a trip to the bathroom. But if his grandfather, or his father, had been behind it, Artemis felt confident that something would have shown up on the man's phone. Abraham and Larry Dawkins might easily have been the patriarchs and brains behind the operation, but Ross was the muscle. The fact that there weren't calls placed to his grandfather from the previous night suggested to Artemis that either Ross had another phone she hadn't found, or else he wasn't involved in the way she had first hoped.

It was all degrees of black. Guesswork. Percentages. She didn't know what to think.

It was certainly still possible that Ross had another phone or had used some sort of code. But going through the man's device, she was finding this more and more difficult to believe.

She scowled, trying to think from another angle. She shifted uncomfortably in the front seat of her vehicle, glancing once more across the lake.

At last, regarding the faintly cracked window, she exhaled deeply, allowing her breath to escape out the gap above the glass.

She should have known.

Things were never this easy.

Ross wasn't behind it. He had decided to take his shot at her in prison, because in his mind, she wasn't only the daughter of the man who had killed his grandmother, she was also a murderer herself. That amount of hatred, over all those years, yielded painful consequences.

But now Artemis had to find a new lead. One of the other Dawkins members? Maybe Larry or Abraham. The father and grandfather were the more powerful members. And Larry Dawkins, during her interrogation with Agent Butcher, had seemed all too excited to find a way to put her behind bars.

But that could easily have been a result of his feelings towards her rather than any participation he had in the ruse.

Which left her with another thought. Was it *really* a ruse? Was she somehow forgetting what had happened?

It seemed an insane proposition. But part of her couldn't help but consider it. It had seemed so real. She had remembered that conversation, the exchange of words. Had remembered the exact phrasing, and even the way Azin had been sitting on the couch.

She paused now, frowning. No. No, she trusted her memory over that camera. Which meant Azin hadn't just been involved but had been *eagerly* involved. She lowered the phone, considering this angle. Azin had acted the part. If her theory was correct and a second video had been recorded after she had left, uploaded to the security company's servers, serving to confuse her and authorities, then Azin had played his part. Using the proper sentences, sitting in the right place on the couch.

Azin had been a part of this, whatever *this* was.

Stupid... she thought to herself. She had been trying to go after an unknown quantity, when she should have just focused on the known quantity. Azin. It was true, he had ended up dead. Confirmed by multiple sources, though, she hadn't seen the body herself. But it was his blood on her sleeve.

She thought back and realized, with a sinking sensation in her stomach, that she could practically remember the moment when he leaned across, his hand brushing her arm. She had been so frazzled by his accusations, his threats, she hadn't realized what he had been doing. But now it made sense. Planting the blood. His own blood. He must have wiped it on her sleeve.

Which meant Azin had been fully in on it. There were no other options. She had narrowed it down. This was the only possibility. And if Azin had been in on it up to his neck, then that meant he was the one she should be investigating.

She hadn't ever investigated a dead man before. The fact that it was a dead chess master hit a little too close to home. Part of her was still thinking about the upcoming bracket tournament.

But it seemed such a small, frail thing compared to everything else.

She thought of Helen. Of those openings her sister had sent her. Some strange sort of code. She thought of Tommy, impossible Tommy, demanding a thousand bucks in exchange for that strange letter in his possession.

She gripped the steering wheel now, and her heart pounded. She knew what she had to do. She put the vehicle in gear, pulled out of her parking spot, and moved up the lakeside road. The moon was starting to dip in the sky, and only a couple of hours of pure darkness remained. It was only about a half hour drive from the lake to the murder victim's house. She had already made the journey once, the previous night.

This time, as she hurtled through the night, she kept to the speed limit as best she could. Her eyes on the road ahead of her, watching for deer that might jump from behind trees or attempt to cross the path in front of her. Azin had been involved. One way or another, he'd been a part of all of this, unwitting or not. And while she couldn't interview a corpse, she could look around his house. Maybe even recover a video file herself. She wanted another look at the security footage. A look in which she wasn't shocked, distracted by what she saw.

And while she could occasionally play detailed memories, especially those she had categorized for her recollection, nothing beat watching the footage in actual high definition.

She tucked her tongue inside her cheek, determined to see this through. Azin was the key. His place would have to be the linchpin to all of this.

Chapter Thirteen

Artemis ducked under the caution tape outside the crime scene. She had managed to slip past the police officer who had dozed off in his car one block down. And now, she moved towards the oceanside house, the scent of salt on the breeze.

As she emerged on the other side of the crisscrossing caution tape, she went still.

A sound caught her attention from around the side of the house. She froze, and a figure emerged.

The figure went still. So did she. They stared at each other. Artemis felt a flash of fear, of embarrassment, of confusion.

Agent Forester jammed his hands in his pockets, scowling at her. He shifted uncomfortably for a moment, and briefly, he seemed at a loss for words.

This was a first, and Artemis didn't want to waste the opportunity to get the first word in. At least, by setting the tone, she wouldn't have to endure five minutes of wisecracking. "Forester," she said simply. "Good to see you." She wanted to add more, to apologize, to excuse herself, to yell at him, all of them. Instead, she just hesitated. "What are you doing here?" she said simply.

Forester tapped his fingers against his large forearm. He considered the question, hesitated, then raised an eyebrow, watching her. "It occurred to me," he said hesitantly, "that the best way to help a friend of mine was to go to the scene of the crime. This is me, here, at that scene."

Artemis scratched at her sleeve, her fingernails finding only fabric and yet finding something soothing about the motion. "You got away?"

He made a dramatic gesture with both hands, which didn't need the accompanying "Voilà!"

She winced. One of her hands pressed against the caution tape behind her. She shot a quick glance towards the sealed door to Azin's house. "I didn't mean to..." She trailed off.

"Abandon me to the wolves?" he said, conversationally. He smiled at her.

The look of amusement flashed in his eyes, all along his face. It was so strange to see, especially because she now had glimpses of what lurked beneath. One part mischievous, humorous, two parts lupine, feral and extraordinarily dangerous.

"I didn't think of it as abandoning you," she said, stilted. "If I'm honest," she said, trailing off. But then she scowled at him and said, "You scared me." The words were vulnerable, the tone was accusatory.

Forester blinked. He hesitated, opened his mouth, and closed it again.

Artemis wasn't sure what to make of the man. In a way, she was touched that he had continued the investigation without her, on her behalf. Even after she had left him behind. A confusing man, this.

But she remembered what he had said; remembered other things he had said over the months she had known him. She also remembered her father, digging at Forester, whispering about knowledge he had.

Artemis pointed at Cameron, and then, her tone firm, she said, with iron in her voice, "I don't know who you think I represent to you, though, it seems as if I must remind you of someone you lost; is that right? Someone who was dear to you?"

He considered this for a moment, still leaning against the wall, his tall, handsome frame drawing her eye, but she refused to allow her gaze to linger.

Forester said, simply, "You remind me of the only person I ever loved." He smiled again, as if the transparency itself was some sort of shield. "When she died, my heart did. Now, sometimes, when I see you, they echo. That enough of an explanation for you, Checkers?" His tone was playful but also acidic. There was an undercurrent of threat to his words. Not quite a threat against her. At least, it didn't feel like it. But rather a threat of knowledge. A sort of implied warning, that if she pried too much, that if she pushed him too far, he would tell her *everything*. Things she didn't want to know. Things he didn't want her to know.

He had the tone of someone suggesting she ought not push him any further.

She chose to acknowledge that tone and said, simply, "Whoever I remind you of, I'm not her. I barely know you. And I'm grateful for your help, but you scared me back there."

"I'm sorry—"

"I'm not finished."

He went quiet.

"If it ever happens again," she said simply, "I'll refuse to speak to you for the rest of my life. Is that clear? Never do something like that again."

Forester just watched her. He didn't reply, just remained leaning against the wall. Then, he cleared his throat, and the spell was broken. He raised his hand like a child in a classroom as if trying to draw her attention. Then, he said, "Excuse me, but when you say never do something like that again, do you mean threatening the guy who tried to kill you *or* just stomping his stupid mug?"

Artemis considered this. And then she said, simply, "I don't like being scared by people who say they are my friends. I have enough people in my life who frighten me. I don't need more."

Even as she said it, she wanted to wince. It sounded so petty, so self-absorbed. As if she was somehow the center of the universe and others had to cater to her emotional needs. She sounded pathetic. She hated hearing the words come from her lips. But this was another problem with Forester. She didn't know how to communicate what she really wanted. She wanted him to be safe, tame, someone she could trust and rely on.

You want him to be Jamie, her mind whispered.

She scowled at the thought. Forester most certainly was not Jamie Kramer. And yet it was Forester standing outside the murder scene. And despite her harsh words, her ultimatum, an attitude that most men might have called bossy or presumptuous, Forester just shrugged and said, "I solemnly swear to be less spooky."

Then, he slipped around the side of the house and disappeared again. From the dark, around the corner, he said, "Front door's locked. Side door's open. Someone threw a brick through the window."

She sighed, and judging by the company, she had little doubt the source of the thrown brick.

Still, though she didn't feel good about following Forester again, she felt a little less terrified.

And sometimes, she supposed that was all someone could ask for. *Less* terrified.

She hastened along the side of the house, inhaling the ocean air, glancing towards the parked police car a block away. The lights were still dim, the lump behind the front seat was still motionless.

"You didn't hurt the cop did you?" she said suddenly.

Forester paused, brushing some glass with his foot and pushing the door open with his elbow. "I didn't kill a cop," he shot back.

"Just asking."

"Checkers, you really are something, you know that? Most people don't have as many constructive criticisms for someone helping to save their life."

Artemis returned one of Forester's trademark smiles. She didn't feel it, and, in fact, nothing about the moment amused her. But it seemed like the right thing to do. He raised an eyebrow at the smirk. And she said, "I guess I'm just one of those girls."

And then, as if somehow she had said something profound, she slipped past him. And only as she moved into the dark space, did the feeling of dread return.

She recognized the scene. Recognized the furniture.

The same red couch where Azin had sat, watching as she approached. The same bookcase off in the corner. But now... red stains on the couch, spilling to the carpet.

She shivered. "We're sure it was Azin, right?"

"Very," Forester said. "Wanna see pics?"

"Umm... Not really." But she didn't look away as Forester raised his phone for her to study. A cold slab, coroner's photos. She winced at the dead man, his chest open, his eyes sealed shut. She looked away. "That's him," she whispered.

"Blood match. Dental match," Forester read the coroner's report. "Poor chess master. So..." Cameron glanced around. "You were standing about where when you shot him?"

"Funny."

"Just checking."

Artemis moved into Azin's rental. Forester moved off to the bookcase. "Do they have his phone?" she said suddenly.

Forester nodded. "Yup. Butcher does."

Artemis paused, lingering near a stack of chess opening pamphlets on a tree-shelf with slanted sections upholding tomes and books and smaller items. "Butcher..." she said. "You seemed to know her."

"Yeah, good agent. Good work. Lousy screw. She kisses and tells, mark my words."

Artemis shook her head. She moved away from the bookshelf, stepping into a small, side room. No bed, just a mattress on the floor. An open suitcase. He hadn't even unpacked. "Do you make a habit of trying to screw your coworkers?" she said. She hadn't realized she was speaking loudly, though.

Forester replied. "Wasn't me coming on to her. She asked me." Forester paused by the couch, shot a look through the open door where Artemis lingered. He shrugged. "Was during a low point in my life. I caved. Was drunk. Pretty sure she took advantage of me." He gave a dramatic sniff.

Artemis shook her head. "I don't think that's funny at all."

"Relax, Checkers. It was mutual. Don't worry about it, alright? I get it—loud and clear. You and boy-wonder are a thing. I won't intrude. Scout's honor."

Artemis turned back to the mattress, hesitating for a moment. She tried to think about what she knew of Azin. An aggressive opener, but a man who *always* prepared standard lines. Notorious for studying every opening his opponents used and memorizing as much counter-play as possible.

As she considered this, she glanced along the floor. Her gaze lingered by the suitcase. She approached, peering inside.

Some disheveled clothing. A soap container. A toothbrush. Her eyes moved past the wall. An outlet extension, with two cables.

She glanced across the room. Another cable where a computer might have gone. But the computer was missing.

"Did they take his computer also?" she called out.

"Yup," he called back. "Find anything?"

"No… well…" She hesitated, frowning. "How many phones did they take?"

"Umm… Only logged one from Azin's. Why?"

Forester's head popped through the door. Artemis pointed at the outlet. "Two chargers," she said. "Different types. One looks way cheaper than the other. No phones though."

Forester approached, studying the two chargers. "Huh…" he said. "This one matches my phone." He wiggled the white wire.

Artemis nodded. "Probably for the smartphone… Which one did they confiscate?"

"Dunno. I just have the list logged. Butcher still plays things close to the vest."

Artemis nodded slowly. "Do you have the footage, per chance?"

"Nope. Butcher."

"Right…" Artemis turned back, glancing at the computer charger across the room, then back to the *two* phone chargers. Different USBs on both of them. Which meant…

"You're sure they only found one phone?" she murmured.

"Mhmm."

Artemis dropped to a knee, next to the chargers. She stared at the two USBs. One was slightly bent towards an end table. The other, cheaper cord, however, was bent towards the bed.

She hesitated, then, frowning, slipped her fingers under the mattress.

Azin always came prepared. And he was particularly skilled at revealed skewers. Hiding a piece behind another *until* he was ready to attack.

"What is it?" Forester asked, his shadow stretching over her.

Artemis didn't reply at first, her fingers probing along the fabric at the base of the mattress... "When we were little," Artemis murmured, "And Tommy wanted to hide things... he thought he was being very clever by securing them *inside* his mattress. Helen found everything though... and... Ah! There!" She felt a surge of triumph as her hand moved, emerging from a slit in the base of the mattress, pulling some cotton fluff past the rigid springs.

But with the cotton came a small, flip cell phone.

Artemis held it up, wiggling it for Forester to see.

He whistled softly.

"Well... nice eye, Blythe. Er, am I allowed to compliment your eye?"

Artemis was in too good a mood to be irritated. She shot back, distracted, "Eye is fine. But do you know any adjectives besides *nice*?"

"Umm... good? Good eye. Hehe. I sound Australian—hear that? Good eye. Like, good day but—oh, shit, what?"

His prattling cut short as he watched her react. Artemis wasn't listening, though. She had opened the phone and was staring at the most recent number. As she did, she nearly dropped the device.

Forester leaned in. "What?" he repeated.

She just stared at the number on the screen. At first, it hadn't meant anything. But then a memory flitted back. She knew *she'd* seen that number before. She could remember when.

Could remember where.

"That's... not... possible," she whispered.

"What is it?" Forester demanded.

Artemis just shook her head. She closed her eyes, desperately thinking. Her body felt numb. Prickles erupted up her arms, down her spine. Fear came in strange, cold spurts.

"Not possible..." she repeated like a broken record.

"Artemis?" Forester said, his tone serious now. "What is it? Do you recognize a number?"

Artemis stared at the phone, stared at the number. She shook her head. Her voice came low, strangled, far too tinny to her own ear. "I... I don't understand," she whispered.

"What?"

"It's... It's the woman I rescued."

"Hmm?"

Artemis raised the phone, wiggling it now, like an accusing finger. "The woman who called me back. The woman I loaned my phone to! God dammit, Forester! It's that woman from the farm! From the Wishing Well Ranch. Holy shit—it's her! She's doing this. She's behind this!"

"Whoa, calm down. What woman, Artemis?"

Artemis was panicking now, stalking back and forth, trying to make sense of it. Prickles spread along her scalp, down her arms. She was shivering now but barely noticed. She could remember that horrible scene, on their last case, in the basement of the burnt-out ranch.

One of the victims, the Professor had trapped inside a metal locker. He'd kept her in there, and Artemis had managed to find her, to free her.

But Wade and Forester had been in a standoff in the barn with a ranch hand by the name of Jeb Arthur. So Artemis had run to help them.

She'd left the woman she'd rescued by a wooden fence. Artemis had even *loaned* her phone to the woman.

"The Professor's victim!" Artemis yelled, waving the phone around now. "That woman. The one from the farm. The one who I leant my phone but who ran away."

Forester blinked. "Wh... it... holy hell."

"Exactly. What the actual fu—"

"Come on... Are you sure it's the same number?"

"Dead sure!" Artemis said. "I don't have my phone to prove it—just this burner Jamie loaned me. But yes. I remember numbers, Forester. It's kind of my thing."

"How do you know it's her number?"

Artemis trailed off. Her lips felt numb. "Because she texted me," Artemis whispered. "After the case. She texted me, letting me know she was okay. But of course... how did she have my number?" Artemis was now hitting her forehead with a closed fist. "Stupid... so stupid. I've been distracted. Blind!"

"What is it? Artemis—*what*?"

"That woman," Artemis spat. "She must have gone through my phone. It's the only way she would have known my number so soon. My private number. She found it because I *gave* it to her."

"She had your phone? Like, unlocked?"

"Yes!" Artemis yelled. "Which means... Oh shit..." The terror had now faded to absolute awe and horror. "She knew my contacts, Cameron. She knew everyone in my phone. She must have been watching Jamie! Sophie! Dear God, that's how she knew about my Christmas sweater. She was wearing the same damn sweater in the video, Forester."

"Shit."

"Shit's right." Artemis was shaking her head, pacing. "She could easily have gotten my fingerprints from my phone, too!"

"Hang on. Listen to yourself. To get your fingerprints? To get all that information? She would have had to premeditate. *Want* to screw you over. Why would she want that? You rescued her!"

"Unless I didn't."

Silence. A pin drop would have been heard.

"What?"

"Unless... I didn't!" she said firmly. "What if she was a plant?"

"How so? The Professor? That acid-flinging bastard?" Forester adjusted his eyepatch, wrinkling his nose.

"Yes!" Artemis exclaimed. "He's like my Dad—he's always up to something. He even claimed to have been involved with my father..."

"Involved... right... I remember. Shit. So you think the Professor put this girl up to it?"

"Or my Dad," Artemis shot back. She gripped the phone in fury. "I should have known it was him!"

Forester gave a faint whistle. "That's some next level screwy, though. To plant someone in order to get something from you? And for her to improvise to steal your fingerprints from your phone?"

"Not just that, though... That was probably a happy accident. She got my contacts, Forester. Everyone I care about."

"Damn. She has my number?"

"Yes! Wade's too!"

Forester just looked pleased that in his equation she'd just said she cared about him. She didn't have the heart or the attention span to correct him. Instead, she said, voice rising, "Other stuff was on my phone. Social security. Address... Birth date. Digital signature... All of it."

"The sort of stuff you might need to register for a firearm?" Forester said innocently.

Artemis shook her head, trying to think back to that moment on the side of the dusty farm road. She couldn't quite picture the woman. She'd had her hair in front of her face. Dirt-streaked, frightened, eyes downcast...

Could *she* have been the actress in that murder video?

The answer was obvious. A resounding *yes.*

It was the same woman... The woman she'd been scared the Professor had taken. The woman Artemis thought she'd *rescued.*

But no... No, the phone number in Azin's phone proved it. Somehow, the Professor had gotten to Azin. Maybe with threats, maybe with bribery... Whatever the case, he'd used this woman to do it. He'd been thinking steps ahead. The woman had been a Trojan horse. A plant. Someone to get near Artemis, to compromise her.

And Artemis had given that woman her damn phone!

Now, she actually did scream at the ceiling.

Frustration, anger, fury all burbled up at once.

The Professor... her father...

They were the same type of evil. The same type of manipulators. "Cameron," she said, stunned... "I... I don't know how to prove it... They covered every base. They... they set me up." She felt weary all of a sudden, her hand falling to her side. She stared off towards a window, skin prickling.

Forester studied her. Then he reached out. His calloused fingers grazed her smooth palm as he took the phone.

He said, quietly, "I can think of one way to find this woman."

"What are you—"

And he dialed her number, turning away from Artemis, raising the phone to his cheek, and waiting for the call to connect.

Chapter Fourteen

Artemis just stared at Forester, unsure what to do. She wanted to slap the phone out of his hand... but why?

He was right. This was the best way to find the perpetrator. At least... if her theory held true. But she was pulling threads to their very distant ends... Out here, so far from the origins of her troubles, things looked murky, as if peering through a glass darkly. She didn't know what was true. Had she deluded herself completely? Was she on the right path?

Forester turned the phone on speaker, and the two of them stood in the quiet murder scene, listening as the call connected.

And then a pause. A voice.

"Hello? Agent Forester?" said the voice. A pleasant, polite voice. An inquisitive, curious voice. Forester raised an eyebrow, glancing at Artemis.

"I take it you got my number from Ms. Blythe's phone," Forester said slowly.

"Yes!" the woman exclaimed, delighted. "Good for you. Well done. Really, good job. I'm very impressed, Cameron. I'm guessing she's there with you?"

"Who?"

"My sister, Artemis. Is she there?"

It took a brief second for the word to register. But when it did, Artemis' soul nearly collapsed. She stared at the phone in Forester's hand, frozen in place. "W-what?" Artemis whispered.

"Oh, hello—I think I hear her, Forester. Mind putting her on please?"

Forester frowned, gauging Artemis' reaction. He paused. "Mind telling me who this is?" he said.

"Of course. Helen Blythe," she replied. "A pleasure to make your acquaintance. Now, please—if you don't mind. My sister?"

Forester extended the phone, his eyes wide. Artemis took the device, but her hand was shaking so badly, she dropped it.

"No—shit!" she lunged, trying to catch it, but only managed to sprain a finger against the floor. None of this made sense. It couldn't be true, could it? *Helen?*

No... no, the Professor had put the woman up to it. He was playing with her. Toying. She'd asked the Professor right before he'd escaped if he'd killed Helen. He'd turned her on to Tommy. But he'd been the one playing with her.

Artemis *knew* this wasn't Helen.

It couldn't be. She was kneeling on the ground now, having recovered the phone and quickly raising it, pressing it to her ear. "He-hello?" she said.

"Artemis!" the woman's voice said back, genuinely excited. "How are you, dear?" The same inquisitive, curious tone.

The woman's voice was just that. A voice of a woman. Not the voice of the fifteen-year-old girl Artemis remembered... but... close? Could it have been the voice of the same person?

It was too hard to tell. The damn phone's connection wasn't great to begin with.

"Who is this?" Artemis demanded, deciding, much like Azin, to go on the aggressive in her opening when it suited her needs.

"Oh, yes... Sorry," the voice said, laughing faintly. "I imagine you must be in shock. Very sorry, dear sister. Very, very sorry about all of this. It will be explained shortly, I'm sure. How are you, though?"

"No. No, shut the hell up. Cut that out. Who is this, *really?*"

"I told you..." the voice said hesitantly, as if mildly offended. "Helen. Helen Blythe. Your sister."

"Not possible."

"Is too."

"How old are you?" Artemis shot back.

"Rude."

"Quick!"

"Thirty-five."

Artemis blinked.

"As of this September, in fact," the woman said.

Both points were accurate.

The woman continued now, a sort of sing-song way. "I remember most things, Artemis. I know you broke father's favorite recliner when you were eight. We blamed Tommy."

Artemis snapped, "Shut up. Someone told you that."

"Oh?" an amused chuckle.

"Who is this really?"

"This is becoming tiresome, sister."

"Stop calling me that!"

A long sigh. "What do you want me to tell you?"

Artemis hesitated. Then she said, "The letter you gave Tommy. What was it?"

"I..." A pause. A moment of hesitation and Artemis felt a surge of triumph. "Perhaps..." The woman on the phone paused, "if you could help me remember... What letter, exactly?"

"Ha!" Artemis declared.

"No, no, one moment," the woman said quickly. "I can tell you more. When you were five years old you fell in love with Jamie Kramer."

"Everyone knows that!" Artemis shot back. Which wasn't strictly true. Whoever this charlatan was on the phone, she'd clearly been put up to it by the Professor. She'd hidden in that horrible, metal coffin, waiting for Artemis to rescue her. And then she'd gone through Artemis' phone. Had that been the plan all along? Artemis scowled in frustration, trying desperately to remember the woman from the side of the road.

Had it been Helen?

Artemis' eyes narrowed. No... no, it wasn't possible. Then again, she could remember the woman's downcast gaze. Her stilted words. Her face streaked and muddy, her hair tangled, matted. Helen had always had such lovely, bronze curls, but the woman from the ranch had such greasy hair, it had been hard to tell.

But no. "Fine," Artemis said simply. "The letter you gave Tommy at the waterfall. A code. What was it?"

A huff of frustration. Some of the polite, collected tone left in a hiss like steam.

"I never gave our brother any letter," the woman on the phone snapped suddenly. And it was as if a spell had been broken, her emotions suddenly getting the better of her act. And Artemis was reminded of another encounter with a similar chameleon. The Professor, when they had found him in his home, had done his best to pretend he was polite, civilized. But when finally confronted with his actions, something had snapped. She could still remember the way he had changed, his posture, demeanor, even something about his facial features rearranging. Like a snake shedding its skin.

"The Professor told you to do this," Artemis said, slowly. "This is a set-up."

The anger faded from the tone and gave way to a playful chuckle. "Of course this is a set-up, dear sister."

"Why?" *Stop calling me that*, she thought to herself. But now, she was sure this woman wasn't Helen. But that didn't mean she could let the question go. She still needed to find out what the woman was up to.

"I would have thought the answer was obvious," the voice said, simply.

"Maybe you should explain it to me," Artemis snapped. She felt as if her emotions were going to war with her mind. She was finding it difficult to focus, to think clearly. The Professor, and whoever else was involved in this horrible ruse, had clearly intended it to haunt her.

And they had gotten what they wanted. She was spinning, kneeling in the dark rental unit, trying to ignore Forester, who watched her like a hawk.

"Artemis," said the woman, "really, you need me to explain it to you?"

And suddenly, Artemis snapped her fingers. "I remember that video," she said, angrily. "An interview I gave in my earlier days. I mentioned my sister's birthday was in September. You could've found that online, too. But I also remember the question they asked!"

"And what question is that, Art?"

"Don't call me that," she said, a growl to her voice. But Artemis didn't continue, preferring to kneel, scowling. She played the interview back in her mind. It had been in her mid-twenties, during an earlier part of her career. After a tournament in which she had drawn the final match, she had been asked about her inspiration. Asked why she had gone for the draw instead of the win. And she had said, *one enemy at a time.* The same phrase the woman in the video had used.

Artemis felt chills along her arms. That video had been from years ago. And yet that was how the woman in the video, the one who had killed Azin, had undoubtedly learned about Artemis. The woman on the phone, in the Professor's employ, had researched her thoroughly. Had gone back years to do it. This realization sent shivers down her arms.

"What do you want?" Artemis said, more firmly. Now that she knew what was happening, she found it easier to breathe. The real trick, she realized, was finding out a way to prove it, to clear her name.

"Think, sister," said the woman. "What do you think I want?"

"I'm not going to play this game with you," Artemis snapped.

"And yet here we are, playing. And in a way, that has always been the point, hasn't it?"

"What does the Professor want?"

A light, airy laugh, contemptuous. "The Professor? He doesn't have anything to do with this. He doesn't even know I'm still alive."

This struck Artemis as an odd comment. Her head was hurting. She didn't know what to say, what to do. "Obviously, you work for the Professor," Artemis said. "That's why you hid in that metal coffin. I thought I was rescuing you, but you were setting me up."

"No, no, it isn't like that. I saw my opportunity to get close to you. I wanted to see what you were like after all these years. It has been so very long. The Professor, if that's what he's still calling himself, though, it's a bit heavy-handed if you ask me... anyway, what was I saying? Right. The Professor hid one of his victims in that box. I found her; she was already dead, and so I moved her. And I took her place, because I knew you would find her."

"The box was locked," Artemis snapped.

"I didn't go through the opening, I went through the hinges. You didn't notice, but the hinges were detached."

"What about the poison on the handle?"

"What about it? I can't solve all of your problems, Art."

"You're not Helen," Artemis snapped. "Stop calling me Art. And just tell me what you want."

A pause, a steady inhale, and then, "A family reunion. I feel quite badly how everything ended. I have been, how do I put this delicately, somewhat in danger myself. A hostage, you might say. But now, I'm starting to feel free again. My captor has lost their edge. I will admit, they put up a very good fight but –"

"You fought the Professor?"

"I really wish you would stop asking me about him. He is old news. Soon-to-be fertilizer. He's a has been, a nothing. Forget about him. He had his uses, but those are over. No, my hostage taker was far more formidable than that old predator."

Artemis was still struggling to make sense of any of this. Her mind kept protesting against the information. Obviously, the woman was lying through her teeth. But parts seemed true. Artemis just couldn't make out which. In a way, it was almost worse than feeling as if she was being lied to completely. One thing was certain, this woman was not Helen. She had done some research, learned some stories, and perhaps, even spoken to her father in prison. Artemis made a mental note to get Forester to look into all the visitors the Ghost-killer had seen, not just recently, but over the course of years.

Her father was behind this... she knew he was. And yet she couldn't help but feel drawn in by the woman's words, lulled into some strange enchantment.

Artemis pushed to her feet, the phone glued to her cheek. She barely even realized she'd brushed past Forester as she approached the window, peering through the glass at the moon-streaked cop car across the road. The man still wasn't moving.

Artemis frowned.

"Now," the voice on the line was saying, "I need you to listen close, sister. This part is very important. At this point, you have to realize that I've won. Even if they *do* believe you. If they believe that somehow this was all a set-up, you won't be able to prove it. All it takes is one prosecutor, one DA, one person to get justice for Azin. For one of the Dawkins to get justice for their grandmother..." A pause, a chuckle. "I think you know where I'm going with this."

"You're blackmailing me," Artemis whispered. "That's what this is about, isn't it?"

"Yes."

The word lingered. Artemis huffed. She felt the same chill along her skin. "What do you want from me? What exactly?"

"You have gotten stupider over the years, Artemis, haven't you?"

"You don't even *sound* like Helen. I remember my sister's voice. I remember her inflections. How she spoke. The phrases she used. You are *not* Helen!"

"I am!" the sudden screech from the phone was so loud, so *feral*, Artemis actually yelped in surprise.

She emitted an unbidden, unwanted sound but cut it off just as quickly. She stared at Forester, eyes wide, heart pounding.

The woman on the other line cleared her throat, inhaling slowly, exhaling. A pause. "My therapist," the woman said softly, "says I need to get control of my emotions. At least... she *used* to say that. Worthless harpy is now feeding maggots in a ditch." A faint sigh. A pause. "You know... I always did hate you, Artemis," the voice murmured. "Always. You were so... innocent. Naive. You thought you were so clever. Helen thought you were the star and the moons!"

Artemis said. "*Helen* thought? You're not my sister. But you knew her! Who are you? Someone from school? A friend of Helen's? Is that it... you're jealous, aren't you?" A pause. A horrible dreadful pause. Then, the tone of her voice as rigid as tombstones, she murmured, "Did you kill my sister."

"I am your sister," the woman snapped back.

But Artemis pressed, feeling cracks. The woman had gotten emotional, lost her temper. The best time to press an advantage was when an opponent was emotionally distraught. To target the weaker portions of their psyche.

In a game like chess, that often meant taking her opponents deep. Using her youth, her endurance, against them. But with someone like this?

This person... this woman on the phone... whoever she was, whatever she claimed to be—clearly she thought a lot of herself. Her ego was practically bleeding through the phone. And so Artemis attacked where the woman felt strongest but was actually weakest.

"You can't be Helen," Artemis said. "You're not smart enough."

A long pause. This time, Artemis thought the woman might have hung up. Then, a shaky inhale.

"What did you say?"

"You heard me. You're not smart enough. I know exactly what you did. Every step. You recruited Azin to start. You... threatened him? Seduced him—though, you were quite a plain woman if I remember."

"You don't remember what I look like," the woman snapped. "I was hiding my face. Otherwise you would have known I was your sister."

"You're not. I know you're not." And as Artemis said it, she felt a surge of confidence. This woman was trying to steal what Artemis valued most. But she couldn't—yes, perhaps she'd heard some rumors, interviewed someone about Artemis. Perhaps she'd even talked to Artemis' father, prying into secret childhood details. But this was not Helen.

Helen had been kind. Compassionate. Extremely intelligent and the prettier and smarter of the two sisters. Only five years Artemis' senior, Helen had treated Art like a best friend. The two had been inseparable, had deeply *loved* each other.

No amount of lies, of tricks, of smoke and mirrors would take that away. How many times had Helen been there? A comforting, kind presence. Helen had smiled often. Her eyes had twinkled. She had spoken with laughter behind her words but also knew when to be solemn or considerate.

Helen... in many ways, had been a role model. Even now, Artemis thought back to her fifteen-year-old sister. The pang in her heart had never lessened.

But this pang alone, this deep sense of vibrant hurt was what told Artemis the woman on the phone was *not* Helen. No matter what she tried.

Couldn't be.

The pain Artemis felt was only the sort that existed in love. Only the sort that was, truly, a felt affection.

No...

Helen might have known this woman. Might even have been... God forbid... *killed* by this woman. But this was not Artemis' sister.

And as she thought it, a slow burning confidence grew in Artemis' chest. A knowledge as deep as bone. This wasn't her sister.

The thought resounded. It brought hope. Brought life. It resurrected dying memories; an attempt at robbing a childhood for a second instance in the same lifetime.

"Perhaps you did see me," the woman on the phone said, taking the silence as opportunity. "Perhaps I have changed so much, you didn't recognize me. Fair. But no, I did not *seduce* Azin. I paid him. He wanted a green card. Wanted to stay." A scornful laugh. "I promised to marry him, so he wouldn't have to return to that hellish country of his."

Artemis scowled. "You bribed Azin to do what... act this horrible ruse out?"

"Come now, Artemis. You think you're so clever." The words were waspish, cold. "You tell me. What did I do?"

"You..." Artemis stood facing the window, still scowling towards where the police officer was sleeping in the car. The night was silent, save the distant swish of the ocean. It would have been peaceful... in other circumstances. "You bribed Azin. He agreed for whatever reason. Perhaps he didn't like me. Perhaps you convinced him, like the Dawkins family believes, that I'm of bad stock. That I'm like my father. Perhaps Azin couldn't abide the Ghost-killer's daughter... or... perhaps he allowed himself whatever excuse he wanted. The smartest people, often, are the most self-deceived."

"What is that? Gandhi?" The woman said sarcastically.

"Actually, no," Artemis said. "Whoever trusts his own mind is a fool—"

"Proverbs 28:26, I know," snapped the woman. "I have the whole book memorized, sister. Solzhenitsyn too. Same with Descartes. With Russel. *The Republic* was a favorite of mine. We read it together. Don't you recall? That little green tent. Flashlights waving about."

"The tent was red!"

"No. You're thinking of our backyard camping trip. Because you think I learned this information from Dad. Or Tommy. But I'm talking about the sister's trip. The summer weekend. Up into the mountains. Remember now? Hmm? The tent was..."

"Green. Right..." Artemis trailed off. She was troubled again. A green tent... How did this woman know the color of the damn tent? She was right. Artemis had thought the tent was red because it was the time they'd camped with witnesses. Someone this woman might have interviewed or bribed for more information.

But the trip into the mountains. A green tent. No one had been there with them. They'd been alone, isolated. Just Helen and Artemis.

It had been one of Artemis' favorite memories. Only two summers before Helen vanished.

The trouble came back now. The hope slowly fading.

Who *was* this woman?

Chapter Fifteen

Not Helen. Her mind kept protesting. *It* isn't *Helen.* And Artemis knew this was true. But how did this woman know so much? About moments Artemis had shared with her sister alone... about the green tent...

She felt silly briefly, considering what Forester might think. Psychic? No... no. Stupid. No such things. No such things...

But what if... what if this woman had interrogated Helen, had stripped information from her real sister like scaling a fish?

The thought sent shivers up Artemis' spine.

A mentalist never revealed their tricks, and this woman had tricks aplenty. Artemis refused to be sucked in though.

"So go on," the woman said. Some of the amusement, the pretend calm facade had returned, suggesting she knew she'd scored one against Artemis. "How did I do it? Azin was bribed. I already conceded that. Who cares why. Men will do the stupidest things for the worst reasons."

Forester nodded sagely with this, but Artemis felt offended. She thought of Jamie taking care of little Sophie. It all came down to perspective didn't it?

"And so you had him set up a meeting with me," she said, her voice less self-assured, still thinking about that damn green tent. How did she *know*? "He recorded it. You were following me. You must have seen what I was wearing. How you got a matching sweater so fast is impressive."

A chuckle. "For that compliment, I'll give you this one for free. The sweater? Sophie got it from a mother at her school. The same mother handed those things out like tic-tacs. I found one myself. Just sitting there on a bed when the family was out for dinner. They didn't know I was there. I wonder what they'd think if they knew a stranger had slept in their bed?" A faint, giddy chuckle at the hypothetical. The sound made Artemis' skin crawl.

"Hang on. That makes no sense." Artemis leaned forward, her forehead pressing against the cold glass. "You didn't have time to steal a sweater."

"No, dear. You'd been wearing that sweater for days now. I knew you'd choose it, or that stupid little form-concealing, black sweatshirt. Hmm? No? You don't exactly have a large wardrobe, do you, Artemis?"

Artemis grimaced. Had this woman been in her apartment, too? No .... No, Artemis had cameras. And yet still, that sense of violation, of fear lingered. Which, she supposed, had been the point.

Artemis' own curiosity dragged her forward now. "So you guessed what sweater I would wear. You were hiding in a car... Across the street maybe?"

"Ha! Guess again."

"You..." Artemis shivered, remembering that large red couch. The way Azin had been sitting on one side but not quite using the arm rest. Somewhat of an awkward position now that she thought of it.

And then Artemis' eyes widened. He'd been sitting as if to direct her attention away from where the book case met the opposite arm of the couch.

"You were in the room," Artemis whispered. "You were there."

"How else would I have memorized your lines, Artemis? Azin memorized his—genius and all that."

"And so I left."

"You left."

"I tossed the photos he gave me into a bush."

"You did. I was hoping to get better fingerprints from the cellophane wrap around the tube. I knew you wouldn't keep it. But when I went to find it, it wasn't there." The woman sounded puzzled briefly. "Why not?"

"It got stuck in a bush," Artemis said simply. "Now I helped you. That makes us even."

"I'll tell you when we're even. But I'm impressed, sister. You've assuaged my concerns that you aren't the right woman for the job. I take it you know how the blood got—"

"Azin touched my sleeve."

"Yes. And the fingerprint—"

"When you had my phone on the ranch road. Weeks ago. That's how you got my information too. My signature. How you registered the weapon."

"Well..." A pause. Another little laugh. "I am very impressed. Well done, sister."

"And the footage afterwards, with me leaving... that was from earlier. A different camera. The footage from the skit you and Azin reenacted... That was taken *after* the footage of me tossing the tube. You planted the gun once you saw me leave that way."

"So you've figured it out. I must commend you. But this all leaves us with—"

"No, hang on," Artemis said. And now she was snapping her fingers, pointing at Forester, gesturing quickly. Artemis handed her own phone to him. Mouthed the word, *record*. And raised her eyebrows.

Forester nodded quickly. Artemis stepped away from the window, just in case—an abundance of caution. She waited as Forester fumbled, clicked the recording button and then raised it near the microphone.

Then, Artemis cleared her throat as if she'd simply paused for dramatic effect. "You skipped over the worst part," Artemis said.

"What? Staining your precious sweater?"

"Killing Azin."

"Oh... Right. Ha. Forgot. You should have seen the look on his face... But no. You did, didn't you? Shocked. He thought we were playing. Thought we were going to blackmail you. I convinced him you had more money than he knew what to do with. Green card. Greens. Greedy, little bastard. Is that why you shot him, Artemis?"

"Wait... No—I didn't shoot him." Artemis glanced at the recording device, frowning.

"No? Because that's what it shows on camera... Also, know what else my camera shows? Hmm? It shows that big galoot next to you trying to record this conversation." A sudden spurt of scorn. "How stupid do you think I am?"

Artemis whirled about, looking at the ceiling, at the bookcase. And then she spotted the faint, blinking light staring right at her. The same camera used to frame her. Now betraying her again.

They were being watched.

Artemis felt a chill down her spine, staring at the camera.

"Smile," the woman whispered. "So, Artemis, tell him to turn off the phone... yes, there we go."

Forester raised the device and complied with the directive.

The woman continued. "Even if you did record it... what does that prove? You hired a voice actor to lie for you? All of this brings us to the truth of the matter. I have you trapped. You are going to spend your life like father is."

"He's not your father."

"Trust me. I wish he wasn't. But I was telling you the truth. I want a reunion. All of us. Like it used to be."

"What are you saying," Artemis snapped, feeling the prickles turn to fear. Cold dread slipped down her spine, along her arms.

"I'm saying, I have a second video. One of Azin and I outlining the plan. Timestamped and everything. I have the other sweater. I have video of the actual murder that *proves* it wasn't you, Artemis."

Thump. Thump. It took a second to realize that Artemis was keeping track of her own heartbeat.

"And you'll release it all? Clear my name? In exchange for what."

"You have connections I don't. Big and gangly next to you is one of them, isn't he? You always had a way with men, Art. Even more than I did."

"I don't understand."

"No? Playing stupid now?" Anger once more. "With your connections, with your ability to come and go as you see fit… Well, you're in the perfect position. You visited him a couple of times already, haven't you?"

"Wh-what?"

"Let me spell it out, since you seem to need the help." The voice grew louder now, as if it had suddenly been pressed tight against the woman's lips. "I want you to free our father. Figure out a way to break Otto Blythe out of prison. In exchange, I'll clear your name. Is that clear enough?" this last sentence was muffled again, suggesting the phone had lowered once more.

Artemis just stared. She didn't know what to say. She stood rooted to the spot, in the shadows by the wall, back to the window. "You want me to…"

"Break father out of prison. Yes. And in exchange, you go free."

"I… I can't do that!"

"You can."

"I won't!"

"You will."

Artemis was howling now. "I would rather *rot* than see him free!"

A deep exhale. "How noble. Even for your own freedom, you won't? I have to say, Artemis, I need you to reconsider."

But Artemis was trembling with rage now. "Absolutely not. I will not free that evil, twisted bastard. He put you up to this, didn't he? The Professor and my Dad. That was the whole plan, wasn't it?"

"Hmm? No. I'm just sentimental is all. Plus... it always was a game between us, Artemis. This was my move. The trick with Azin. Now it's your turn. I duped the FBI. Duped the sheriff's office. Surely you can trick a few prison guards. A warden? By the sound of things you've already cozied up with them, taking some of Daddy's playthings away."

"Stop it! Stop acting like you're Helen. You're a twisted shrew, and I'm *never* going to help Otto. Ever! Do you hear me? I don't care if you had a gun to my head!" Artemis was yelling now, facing the camera she'd spotted. In her anger, she flung the phone across the room. It struck the wall and fell onto the bed.

Artemis pointed at the camera. "Can you hear me? Hmm? Listen close! You think you can threaten my freedom to get me to help Otto? Not a chance. Not even if I was being dragged to hell. He stays where he belongs." She went quiet now, breathing heavily, realizing Forester was holding the phone again, frowning.

Artemis felt sweat on her forehead. She scowled now, twisting uncomfortably where she stood, moving from one foot to the other.

For a moment, a strange, bitter silence reigned. And then...

Bzz. Bzzz.

Forester winced, raising the little phone and wiggling it between thumb and forefinger. "Want me to answer?"

Artemis was still exhaling sharply. She shot a narrow-eyed look at the camera, scowling. Then glanced back at Forester.

She didn't reply. *Bzz. Bzzz.*

A few more rings, then it stopped. The phone went dark.

Forester and Artemis just stood in the bleak space, watching each other. The red light on the camera blinked ever so softly. Without looking directly at it, Artemis realized, she never would have noticed it. Especially not during the day time when the red light was obscured by the normal ambiance of day.

But only a moment passed before the phone continued. *Bzzz. Bzzz.*

Artemis snarled and ripped the phone from Forester's hand. She opened it, screaming, "Go to hell!"

"One moment, sister," the voice came back, cold and cruel. Something about the tone, a whispered tone hinting at absolute control, caused Artemis to go quiet. "Behave now."

"What?" Artemis snapped. "I told you no."

"Plan B, then. You won't fight for your own survival? I can think of someone you might fight for. It was really a very nice sweater. And... oh, look at that. They're still up. Two people in the living room. Nice balloons by the way." And then the woman hung up.

This time she didn't call back.

Artemis stood rooted to the spot for only a split second. And then the horror flooded through her, robbing her of her breath. "Jamie," she whispered. "Sophie... She's going after the Kramers!" She rounded on the tall agent. "Forester! She's going after Jamie and Sophie!" Artemis was now moving, almost stumbling towards the door as if not quite sure which direction to point her feet. "The Washingtons... No... no... They're all there! She's at the ranch!"

And then Artemis spun on her heel and broke into a dead sprint, slamming back through the side door, kicking scattered glass, and racing in the direction of the parked car.

Chapter Sixteen

Forester gripped the plastic handle over the window, his knuckles white, but Artemis didn't slow, testing every speed limit known to man.

"Come on!" she screamed, twisting her fingers against the steering wheel. "Come on... come on!" They raced up the highway, under the watch of the streetlights flashing by. The GPS chirped from where she'd placed it on the dash, sliding across the console and nearly falling before Forester caught it.

"Arriving at destination on left," the voice said, growing fainter as it slipped away across the console.

Artemis aided the device's bid for freedom as she spun the wheel, veering onto the long driveway. "Someone had to be watching the ranch, right?" she was saying, her voice shaking. "They had to be! Why wouldn't the cops watch the ranch?"

"Might have drawn them away with our beat down on Ross," Forester said, grim.

"Your beat down!" she snapped.

"Important right now?"

"No... No... Dammit!"

"Wait—stop—cops!" Forester jammed a finger through the window, and Artemis hit the brakes. It took some time for her to completely process what she was looking at. In the foreground, past the road, parked on the side, near one of the horse paddocks, she spotted the car. What Forester had pegged as a cop car, though, was better described as an undercover police car. Tinted windows, dark paint. Beyond the car, up the long, winding road, settled on top of a small, grassy hill, was the ranch house itself, which Jamie had so proudly shown her not so lo ng ago.

The lights were off, and she spotted no movement in the house. However, even from this distance, it looked as if the front door was open. Artemis felt her stomach twist.

As they skidded, slowing, trying to avoid detection by the police but cutting it far too late, Artemis changed her mind, and she floored the gas, turning back up the road, racing towards the house.

Forester tried to caution her, raising his voice the faster she went. "In the road!" he snapped, "Watch out!"

She had been so focused on the parked car, she hadn't noticed the body in the road. She veered around but already spotted the pool of blood. She caught a glimpse of a pale face, lying against the ground. Pinched features, dirty blonde hair.

Agent Butcher, her throat slit. At least now Artemis knew who that car belonged to.

"Shit," Forester yelled, looking in the rearview mirror at the body in the road.

"I'm sorry," Artemis was saying, "I'm sorry."

The dead woman in the pool of blood didn't move. It was testament to how much people had been screwing with her mind that at any moment, Artemis expected the corpse to rise, to move, to flash a smile and a thumbs up and declare, "Gotcha!"

But it never happened. Sometimes, there was no waking up from a nightmare.

The dead woman was only the harbinger, though.

Dread crawled up Artemis' spine. She slammed the brakes, skidding in the parking space in front of the garage. The pink rental vehicle was still there, belonging to the Washingtons. But there was no sign of Jamie Kramer's favored SUV.

The door slammed. Forester did a three-sixty turn, as if unsure which direction to go. He stared towards the body in the road, twisted, then moved at last to follow after Artemis as she was already sprinting up the stairs.

Trap, a voice whispered in her mind. But she barreled straight through the open door, shouting, "Jamie!"

She stumbled over a second body and nearly fell on top of a third. Two more figures lying in the doorway. Both of them motionless.

The Washingtons, face-down, shattered glass across the ground around them. Red liquid staining the floor.

"No, no, no," Artemis said, her voice shaking. "No... *no*, no!" But her screams didn't matter. The figures didn't move. Glass crunched under foot as she stumbled further into the house. "Henry!" she yelled, "Cynthia!" She dropped to a knee, fingers scrabbling desperately at the two fallen figures.

Neither of them moved.

But then.

A faint sound. A grunt, a breath.

Henry was alive.

And then, as Forester stumbled after her, cursing as he did, he flicked the lights on. The Washingtons were lying amidst red stains... not blood. No. Fruit punch from the big bowl on the table. The shattered glass, from the chalices Jamie had set out for the special occasion, honoring Artemis' achievements.

Artemis' heart pounded, but she felt a flicker of hope.

She flipped Cynthia gently and let out a relieved gasp. The woman was breathing in shallow gulps, but her eyes were closed. Artemis pulled at one eye—the pupil dilated.

"Drugged!" Forester said. "They're both drugged!"

"Call paramedics! Now!"

"Cops will arrest you, Artemis. Me too if Dawkins recognized me."

She whirled on Cameron, staring him in the eye. She opened her mouth but he chastised himself first. "Shit. Yeah, wait. Sorry. Calling." His phone was in his hand and he was hastily dialing 9-1-1.

Artemis heard the three faint beeps.

She double-checked the Washingtons were breathing, placed both of them so the glass wasn't near them, then spun and raced further into the house. "Jamie!" she was yelling. "Sophie!"

But no answer.

The house just echoed with quiet. Artemis stumbled up the stairs, checking the bedrooms in a flurry, like a whirling dervish, tearing through the space.

But nothing. No one was there.

Her heart threatened to pummel the inside of her chest now. She stumbled from one room to the next. Checking the bathroom.

Jamie's room—neat, tidy, clean. Everything arranged perfectly. Sophie's room—pink and blue, horses on the wall, a small barbie sticking out of a dollhouse chimney.

She checked under the beds. In the wardrobes. Nothing.

As she raced back downstairs, checking the first level again, then heading towards the basement, Forester—who was tending to the Washingtons, propping them so they could breathe properly—yelled, "On their way. Artemis, you need to get out of here. I'll handle it. Go!"

"I have to find Jamie! Sophie!" she yelled, louder.

No response.

Forester sat upright, half-kneeling still, but watching her, grimacing. "They're not here. They're gone. Artemis, they're gone!"

"Jamie!" She raced to the basement, kicked the door open. Down the stairs. Peering in the naked space. Jamie had described how he wanted to turn the place into something of a lounge. He'd described a spot for a bookshelf and bean bag for reading. Couches for entertaining guests. Maybe even a movie theater if they could eventually afford it.

But the bare space now only whispered of empty promises and dying dreams.

The Kramers weren't there.

Artemis spun back around, taking the concrete steps two at a time, gasping as she did. She wasn't sure if she was trying to breath or sob.

Jamie didn't deserve this. Sophie didn't either. The two had already been through so much. Her heart shattered for them. Their parents, dead. Their father a murderer. The two of them suddenly severed from their relatives in one fell swoop.

And at the center of it all...

Artemis.

Her father had helped Mr. Kramer. She'd been there when Kramer was shot. And now Jamie and Sophie were... gone.

Again because of her.

"God damn it!" she screamed, stumbling back up the stairs.

In the distance, faintly, she thought she heard sirens.

Forester was now facing her, having hurried over from the Washingtons. He reached out, hands on her shoulders, trying to steady her, to look her in the eyes. "Listen to me," he was saying. "Artemis—hey... hey, please *listen.*"

She sobbed, shaking her head, trembling. "They're gone," she whispered. And though she sobbed, the tears didn't come. Even after all of it, after everything...

The Ghost-killer's daughter still couldn't cry.

She hated herself for it.
She hated herself deeply.

Forester watched her, hands still resting on her shoulders. Strong, comforting hands. Stabilizing hands. And yet she just wanted to collapse. "I c-can't," she stammered. Her stomach twisted. Her chest tightened.

And Artemis' legs gave out.

How pathetic, a scathing voice whispered as she hit the ground. Her head struck hard against the tiles. She spotted the balloons dangling from the ceiling. Spotted the way the ribbons dangled towards her, teasing and taunting like the trailing, fluorescent fingers of some mischief-maker.

But her stomach was now so tight she thought she might vomit.

A panic attack. Her mind registered the assault a second after her body began to convulse.

"Hey, hey," Forester whispered now, dropping his voice, dropping next to her. He lifted his hand, no longer touching her. He tried to calm her. His voice was gentle. "Hey—it's going to be okay. I promise. I won't let them hurt you. I won't let them do anything to you! It's going to be okay!"

She shook, convulsed, gasping but not quite breathing. Hyperventilating, but somehow leaving her lungs depleted.

And as Forester tried to comfort her. Hand occasionally touching her shoulder, or stroking the side of her head, she could hear his voice shaking.

It was hard to make out much. Hard to see when all one could really do was focus on drawing air. Focused on not shriveling up at the core and turning inside out.

But as she shifted on the ground, gasping, groaning, trying to calm down, she caught glimpses of Forester.

The sociopath knelt over her... eyes gleaming with tears. Those same crystal droplets trailed along his cheeks, wobbled on his chin. He stared at her, his voice gentle, his face rigid, but his mask unable to conceal the crying.

Her mind went out from herself. It was because of her own thoughts that her body had collapsed, and so, for a brief moment, she considered Forester...

This man... Anti-social personality disorder, they called it. Sociopaths couldn't cry. *Didn't* cry.

But there he was... tears.

Even a man without a conscience could weep for others...

And all Artemis could manage was to collapse and shake.

Her mind still spun. She wondered, as she lay there on the cold tiles, *who* Forester was looking at. Artemis Blythe... or someone else. Those tears weren't for a colleague he'd met a couple of months ago. No... no, those were tears, precious gemstones, that belonged to someone else entirely.

Someone Artemis had never met.

Someone Forester saw whenever he looked at her, and whenever Artemis cared to pay attention to the odd recognition in his eyes.

And so the agent cried, trying to calm her, to comfort her. But Artemis was beyond consolation.

How could she explain to him?

He kept murmuring, "It's going to be okay... I've got you. I won't let them hurt you."

You. You. You. You.

God damn you.

She didn't care about *you*. Herself. Didn't care if she was protected. Didn't care if she was hurt.

Jamie and Sophie. The Washingtons. The people *she* cared about. Those were the ones that needed help. Not her. Not the Ghost-killer's awful daughter.

She deserved to lie on the floor like this. Deserved to break, to shake, to stare into a dreadful, hopeless future.

In a way, she'd always known despair was her fate.

She'd simply tried to outrun it for a decade or two.

But how does one outrun a thing in their own mind?

Self-pity? Now? How selfish are you?

And so a new salvo of accusation joined the fray. If she didn't cry, she was heartless. If she didn't hope, she was futile. If she didn't rise, she was selfish. Where could one go to properly repent of their very humanity?

She didn't know. And so she tried to sit up.

Sometimes motion was all it took to forget self-loathing.

She propped on her elbow, gasping horribly. Forester tried to help her. She felt one of his tears fall and streak her knuckles. She inhaled, exhaled. He was tapping a rhythm again, trying to give her something to focus on.

But it didn't work.

Nothing worked...

And that's when the phone rang.

Jamie Kramer's phone, an old landline, a rotary phone. It had come with the equally old ranch house. Jamie had thought it quaint.

But now it only conjured dread.

Brrng. Brrrng. Brrrnng.

Artemis listened, focusing on the beeping phone. She tried to rise again, but her stomach was now buckling. She bent double, gasping at her feet. At least she was sitting up now.

How had that happened?

Brrng. Brrrrng. Brrrrrng!

And in the distance now, sirens. Definite sirens. Coming ever closer. Artemis would be sent to prison. Ross Dawkins would testify against her. Breaking and entering... assault... murder... If Ross could testify at all.

By going to his house, had she made things worse on herself?

Plausible deniability. Everyone knew he hated her... Didn't they?

Too many thoughts. Too many tethers. She couldn't hold on.

Brrrng. Brrrrrng. More insistent.

She shoved to her feet, stumbling. She would have fallen if not for Forester. And again, it was Cameron at her side, guiding her forward, towards the phone.

He didn't say a word now, having realized it seemed that it wasn't language she needed in that moment.

She snatched the phone off the cradle, pressing the cold plastic to her face.

The incessant ringing faded.

But the distant sirens continued to draw near.

And then a voice. "Artemis?" Jamie's voice. "Artemis? Are you okay? Hey—hey tell me you're okay!"

She paused. The weight in her stomach lessened a bit. "Jamie?" she gasped, her voice shaking. Forester's hand tensed ever so slightly on her arm, but he didn't let go.

"Jamie!" she yelled. "I'm fine—I'm... The Washingtons..." she swallowed.

"Thank God," Jamie said. "Alright... They should be fine. She said they'd wake up soon enough."

"She? Who? Jamie?" Artemis heart skipped. "Is she there, with you? Is she—"

"Hello, sister," said a new voice. Artemis could hear Jamie in the background, protesting. But then a snarl. "Sit down, or I'll blow her little brains out."

Another yell, then quiet. Sobbing now. Not Jamie.

"Sophie?" Artemis yelled. "You bitch! What are you doing?!"

"I thought it might be obvious," said the woman in a world-weary tone. "We've been over what I want, yes? Now... I have leverage. Leverage you care about, since it seems as if you don't give a damn about yourself, do you?"

Artemis was shaking, leaning against the counter. Forester was now tugging at her, insistently, like a golden retriever pleading to go for a walk.

"Artemis," he whispered. "Please... we have to go. You can't be here. The Washingtons will be fine. *Please.*"

Artemis was still trembling. She pulled her arm away from Cameron. "Let them go! Do you hear me, let them go!"

A pause. No sound. Then, "Who are you addressing, Artemis? It's rude not to use someone's name. Ask me nicely. I'll consider it."

Artemis wasn't going to play though. She certainly wasn't going to call this evil woman *Helen.* "Tell me!" Artemis shrieked. "What do you want? Just let them go. They didn't do *anything.*"

"Huh. You really do care about them. Strange. I would've thought you'd have some of this passion for your own sister. But you did nothing to find *her.* To find *me.* Did you?"

"Please..." Artemis' voice cracked. Was this what it had come to? Begging serial killers on the phone? This woman had already killed Azin, at least. And also Agent Butcher. She'd spared the Washingtons for some reason... Strange... Artemis would have to consider this later. There was a reason, no doubt. This woman was enacting a meticulous plan. Her father's plan? Most likely.

She said the Professor wasn't involved at all... but she had to be lying, right?

Artemis stopped speculating. It was just giving her a headache. She needed more information, but the pursuit of information was what had led her to Azin's in the first place. She felt like a small fly, only now sensing the vibrations that had lured the black widow.

"Look, Artemis, my terms are simple. I have a gun pressed to handsome Jamie's forehead. I know how much you've always liked him. He has nice lips." A chuckle. "You people really are so easy to manipulate. A bit of dust in the punch. A few threats to the child, and everyone does what I say. I threaten his sister, he's like a puppy. I threaten him, and you... well, not a puppy. Maybe... a piglet? A chinchilla? I'll get back to you on the metaphor."

"Just let them go," she pleaded. The sirens were now close. She could see the lights flashing through the glass.

"I told you once," said the voice, cold and certain and clear. "I won't hurt either of them. I'll bring them to you. In exchange."

"I can't," Artemis said. Her voice a whisper.

"Oh? I can't either. Can't seem to stop my finger on this trigger. Uh-oh. Oh no. Oh NO!"

Bang!

A sudden scream. Then silence. The line had gone dead.

"A gunshot," Artemis said. "That was... that was a gun—Forester!" She slammed the phone back on the hook, snapping her fingers. "Her number. What was... oh, right." She played the digits across her mind. How did one dial a damn rotor phone, though?

Before she could call, though, the phone rang again.

Artemis ripped it from the cradle. She yelled, "You monster! What did you do!"

"Nothing, nothing," the woman said, chuckling. I fired into the plaster. It's fine... No—don't try to think where there might be *plaster*, hoping to narrow it down. I promise you I'll be gone before you have a chance to find me. But here, don't trust me? Jamie? Sophie, say hi to little Artemis."

"Artemis?" Jamie said. "Don't do what she wants! Don't do it!"

In the background, Artemis could hear Sophie crying. Her heart twisted. But at the sound of their voices, she found she could breathe again.

"Now," said the woman. "Let's try again, shall we? My finger is on the trigger. Can I or *can't* I? Hmm? I think I can. But I'm not sure. You go first. *Can* you or *can't* you help me?"

Artemis froze in place. The woman wanted the impossible. Wanted Artemis to break her father out of prison. But why?

She shook her head. It didn't make sense. Who was this woman? The Ghost-killer had hired her. It was the only solution. Her father was behind all of this, wasn't he?

"Well?" the woman said. "Can I? Or Can't I? My finger is starting to shake, Ms. Blythe."

Artemis bit her lip, the pain lancing through her. Her hatred for her father had been the strongest thing in her life for years. The only driving force she knew. Bitterness and regret had dominated her heart.

But now...

Jamie. Sophie.

The hand tensed on her shoulder.

She closed her eyes. There were some things stronger than hatred.

Not many. Not very many at all.

"I'll do it," Artemis said, breathing heavily. And as she said it, a sense of relief joined the promise. It felt like ripping a band-aid in one quick yank. "I'll do it!" she said, louder.

"Do what. Be specific," the voice said, cold. "Because if not, *I'll* do it."

"I'll break him out of prison. I promise. I will."

"Break who? Or is it *whom.* I never can remember."

"I said I'll do it. Now let them go."

"No. That's not how this works. The Kramers are going to be my guests. If I think you're trying to find me, Artemis..." Another loud *bang!*

"God dammit!"

Laughing again. "They're fine." But this time she didn't put Jamie on to prove it. "But do I make myself clear? Don't try to find me. Don't talk to the police, except for the big ape who follows you around like a love-struck puppy dog."

Forester's hand lifted from her shoulder, and he swallowed, not quite watching her. Artemis wasn't sure if he'd heard the comment over the muted receiver, or if it had just been bad timing.

She was too distracted to think much on it.

"Don't try to trick me. Don't try *anything*. Or I'll end them both. Remember, Artemis, you're a fugitive. If you give me what I want, I'll release Jamie, release—Sophie, was it?"

"Hey! Hey, don't touch her face!" Jamie yelled in the background.

"Relax. She's got such cute cheeks." A laugh. Then, "And also, Artemis, I'll give you your life back. I'll send proof, incontrovertible evidence that you were *not* Azin's killer. Three for the price of one. Now *that* is a bargain. Can we agree? Hmm? And all you have to do is bring me Dad. Bring me Otto Blythe."

Artemis shuddered again, shaking her head in fury. She couldn't say no, though. She'd already agreed. Both verbally and in her mind. Her heart wanted to protest, wanted to gouge into the earth and refuse to be dragged along with this horrific promise.

But...

Jamie... Sophie...

She bit her lip.

"I'll do it. I said I would."

"Good. You have exactly one week. Use your FBI friend. Use Tommy—he's got contacts. And use that big brain of yours. If anyone can do it, it's you. You always were Dad's favorite. Good luck, sister."

And then the line died.

Artemis held the phone, feeling the plastic cold against her fingers. In the background, through the windows, she heard shouting voices. Loud cries.

"They found Butcher," Forester whispered, his tone calm once more. The tears were gone as if they'd never even been there. Once again, Forester's expression was bland. His words, firm and direct. "If you want to do this," he said, nodding at the phone. "You can't be in prison. So... out the back?"

She stared at him. Listening to the shouts. To the sound of footsteps as paramedics and police, likely both, made their way to the farmhouse.

She shot a quick look at the Washingtons, making sure the couple were comfortable, nowhere near the glass and still breathing.

"They'll be fine," Forester murmured.

Artemis was hyperventilating again.

"They'll be fine," Forester whispered.

He was a quick study. She had to hand him that. No longer attempting to assuage her with *you'll be fine.* But rather, *they'll be fine.*

She could only hope he was right. She gave a quick, stiff nod.

What else was there to do?

Forester took this as permission. He grabbed her wrist and began tugging insistently, guiding her along the hall towards the back of the house. "Hurry," he murmured. "We have to leave the car. Let's go."

"You're coming?" she asked, stumbling now, shooting looks back. The door opened suddenly. The voices spilled into the farmhouse now.

Forester shot her a look and wrinkled his nose as if this was a stupid question. "I told you I wouldn't let anything happen to you," he muttered. "So yeah. Sherlock. I'm coming."

"I don't care if anything happens to me," she whispered.

"I guessed as much. Which is why I'm coming. One of us has to watch your back. Just know," he said, reaching the back door, elbow first, pausing and peering into the dark then easing the door open. Wind ushered through in a puff. "If you keep tossing yourself on other peoples' grenades, Imma get a hernia trying to kick 'em out from under you."

"What?"

"Tried for a metaphor," he muttered. "Come on. Quick—to the trees."

"I liked your dog metaphor better, back in the car," she murmured. It wasn't a very helpful comment. The words meant so little, she forgot them the moment she spoke them. Empty words in an empty space.

Her mind was elsewhere. Distant.

Considering everything she knew about the maximum-security prison. About her father.

And about what she was going to have to do in order to rescue Jamie Kramer and his sister. She stumbled along the rough ground behind the farmhouse. Sirens continued to flash against the sky. Voices on the radio and those in the open air called back and forth.

And together, Forester and Artemis fled into the woods, their shoulders hunched, each encumbered in their own way. But the greatest of burdens was the impossible task.

Within a week, they had to break Otto Blythe, the Ghost-killer, out of prison.

Or else.

The End

What's next for Artemis Blythe?

She Runs Away

If she doesn't break her father out of prison, the man she loves will be killed.

With the help of a wild-card FBI agent and a brother involved with the Seattle mob, Artemis Blythe plans a prison break. But in order to get close to the warden, she promises to solve a twenty-year-old cold case that has baffled the FBI for decades.

Now, the genius FBI consultant must solve the old murder, trick the warden, and—most of all—figure out a way to outwit her father and whoever is behind the diabolical plan to set him free.

Once a hypnotist with her own TV show, now, Sophie Quinn works as a full-time consultant for the FBI. Everything changed six years ago. She can still remember that horrible night. Slated to be the River Killer's tenth victim, she managed to slip her bindings and barely escape where so many others failed. Her sister wasn't so lucky.

And now the killer is back.

Two PHDs later, she's now a rising star at the FBI. Her photographic memory helps solve crimes, but also helps her to *never* forget. She saw the River Killer's tattoo. She knows what he sounds like. And now, ten years later, he's active again.

Sophie Quinn heads back home to the swamps of Louisiana, along the Mississippi River, intent on evening the score and finding the man who killed her sister. It's been six years since she's been home, though. Broken relationships and shattered dreams exist among the bayous, the rivers, the waterways and swamps of Louisiana; can Sophie find her way home again? Or will she be the River Killer's next victim to float downstream?

GIRL UNDER THE ICE

Once a rising star in the FBI, with the best case closure rate of any investigator, Ella Porter is now exiled to a small gold mining town bordering the wilderness of Alaska. The reason for her

new assignment? She allowed a prolific serial killer to escape custody.

But what no one knows is that she did it on purpose.

The day she shows up in Nome, bags still unpacked, the wife of the richest gold miner in town goes missing. This is the second woman to vanish in as many days. And it's up to Ella to find out what happened.

Assigning Ella to Nome is no accident, either. Though she swore she'd never return, Ella grew up in the small, gold mining town, treated like royalty as a child due to her own family's wealth. But like all gold tycoons, the Porter family secrets are as dark as Ella's own.

Greenfield press is the brainchild of bestselling author Steve Higgs. He specializes in writing fast paced adventurous mystery and urban fantasy with a humorous lilt. Having made his money publishing his own work, Steve went looking for a few 'special' authors whose work he believed in.

Georgia Wagner was the first of those, but to find out more and to be the first to hear about new releases and what is coming next, you can join the Facebook group by copying the following link into your browser - www.facebook.com/GreenfieldPress.

About the Author

Georgia Wagner worked as a ghost writer for many, many years before finally taking the plunge into self-publishing. Location and character are two big factors for Georgia, and getting those right allows the story to flow seamlessly onto the page. And flow it does, because Georgia is so prolific a new term is required to describe the rate at which nerve-tingling stories find their way into print.

When not found attached to a laptop, Georgia likes spending time in local arboretums, among the trees and ponds. An avid cultivator of orchids, begonias, and all things floral, Georgia also has a strong penchant for art, paintings, and sculptures. A many-decades long passion for mystery novels and years of chess tournament experience makes Georgia the perfect person to pen the Artemis Blythe series.

Also By Georgia Wagner

Girl Under the Ice

Once a rising star in the FBI, with the best case closure rate of any investigator, Ella Porter is now exiled to a small gold mining town bordering the wilderness of Alaska. The reason for her new assignment? She allowed a prolific serial killer to escape custody.

But what no one knows is that she did it on purpose.

The day she shows up in Nome, bags still unpacked, the wife of the richest gold miner in town goes missing. This is the second woman to vanish in as many days. And it's up to Ella to find out what happened.

Assigning Ella to Nome is no accident, either. Though she swore she'd never return, Ella grew up in the small, gold mining town, treated like royalty as a child due to her own family's wealth. But like all gold tycoons, the Porter family secrets are as dark as Ella's own.